JUST

A

HAT

BOOKS BY S. KHUBIAR

JUST

A

HAT

S. KHUBIAR

**BLACK
STONE**
PUBLISHING

Maybe you are seeking among the branches
what is only found in the roots. —*Rumi*

1
CAT IN THE HAT

The big round white thermometer on Joseph's porch said it was dangerously hot. Ninety-nine degrees. It felt like the red needle was spinning around the black hash marks. Joseph's best friends, Mateo and Roberto Ybarra, worked across the street in the neighbor's landscaping. While their father edged the sidewalk, the twin thirteen-year-olds pulled weeds from the Greers' flower beds. An elegant, metal sign sat enthroned among the dahlias proclaiming: *Hazel, Texas, 1978 Flower Garden of the Year*.

The Ybarras did the work in the Texas summer heat. The Greers collected the award.

"Hey, Mateo," called Joseph from his front porch. "You guys want a sharbet?"

Mateo and Roberto looked up. So did Joseph's father, who was next door remounting Miss Eleanor's mailbox. Baba had told Joseph to take the kitchen trash can outside and clean it after supper. Instead, Joseph lingered to help Maman do the dishes. It gave him the opportunity to remind her that the home-made peach sharbet was frozen and ready. Mateo shrugged and yelled back, "*¿Qué es eso?*"

"*Es como un helado,*" Joseph explained in Spanish, then in English. "Persian ice cream."

Two older boys rode by on their bicycles. They shouted something at Mateo and Roberto as they pedaled by. Mateo watched until they turned at the end of the block before he looked back at Joseph and nodded.

Joseph grinned. He gave his father a glance and went back inside the house. There was plenty of time to clean out the trash can before dark. The twins were going to like Maman's fresh peach sharbet.

Roberto and Mateo looked up eagerly when Joseph emerged from his house. He carried three blue plastic cups filled with sharbet. Baba looked over as well. He called to Joseph in the Persian language, Farsi. "Give some sharbet to Mr. Ybarra, too."

"*Baleh*, Baba," Joseph agreed, and he stepped off the curb. The two shirtless boys on bicycles returned. One of them rode straight toward him. Joseph wasn't sure which way to dodge. The boy suddenly popped a wheelie, barely missing Joseph. The other boy veered off to the other side of the street. He used a stick to scratch the side of Mr. Ybarra's old farm truck as he rode by.

Mr. Ybarra turned to edge back to the street, and he stopped. Roberto and Mateo looked at their dad, who shook his head slightly. He pressed his sweat-stained, straw cowboy hat a little lower and resumed edging.

"Hey!" Joseph yelled after the boy who scratched the truck. "You *pedar sagg!*" He yelled so loudly that Mr. Ybarra looked up again.

"Youssef!" Joseph's father called, using Joseph's Farsi name.

Joseph ignored him. The heat of indignation flamed too high. Both boys turned at the end of the block and pedaled back. Joseph crossed the street to deliver the sharbets, but he watched the shirtless boys approach this time. He was pretty sure they were a couple of years older than him. Joseph wouldn't start eighth grade until this school year.

Roberto and Mateo left their weeding to meet him. Both were sweating, and their hands and the knees of their jeans were covered in dirt. Joseph handed them each a sharbet. As he turned to walk to Mr. Ybarra, one of the shirtless boys darted into the Greers' driveway and skidded to a stop. The boy carelessly threw his bike down and walked to intercept Joseph. What the boy did was so unthinkable that Joseph didn't even try to stop him. After all, Mr. Ybarra was right there on the lawn.

The boy slapped the peach sharbet. He slapped it all the way to the edge of the driveway. The icy, peach treat splattered, some of it on the concrete, some on the freshly cut lawn. Joseph simply stared at the sharbet at first, then he looked at the boy who stood there sneering. "What did you call me, you greasy wetback?" asked the boy. He looked like a possum, narrow-faced with small black eyes.

Joseph stood toe-to-toe with him. Baba was six foot five and Joseph was growing faster than all his classmates. In fact, even though he was skinnier, he was taller than this thug. Joseph's heart pounded. His eyes watered in anger. He leaned in, ready to go.

The other boy rode right up to them both on the driveway. He grinned catlike at Joseph from beneath a dingy Hazel Fighting Hawks ballcap and long dirty-blonde hair. "Look, he's about to cry," the boy said. He sat back comfortably on the bike, propping a foot on the handlebar. The boy looked like an amused tabby watching a mouse.

"No, I'm not," said Joseph. He was frustrated that his eyes sent the wrong signal. "I'm about to . . ."

"Youssef," said Baba. He had crossed the street, and he walked up the driveway.

The two invaders looked back. They stared at the enormous brown man walking toward them. Unlike Mr. Ybarra, Kamran Nissan was not dressed in jeans and a work shirt. He wore clean, pressed khaki trousers and a short-sleeved, navy Lacoste shirt with fine leather loafers. In his hand was a Phillips screwdriver. The cat-eyed boy in the Hawks cap took his foot off the handlebar uneasily.

"Youssef," repeated Baba in Farsi. "Go back home."

"But Baba, they . . ."

"I said go back home. You will do nothing to make anyone call the police." Although Joseph was nearly shaking to take a swing at the possum-faced boy, he obeyed. The Ybarras watched silently.

Baba stood at the end of the driveway until Joseph made it to his own porch. Afterward, Baba walked back to Miss Eleanor's porch to finish mounting the mailbox. The two thugs hurled a few more insults at the twins about how dirty Mexicans needed to go back to Mexico. They rode away, bicycle wheels spinning. That was outrageous. The Ybarra family had been living in Texas since the early 1800s. They were Tejanos. Maybe Joseph was an outsider, but not the Ybarras.

Joseph wanted to go talk to the twins, but from Miss Eleanor's porch, Baba gave him a hand signal. It promised punishment worse than an ear pull if he didn't go inside the house.

This made Joseph so angry that his stomach hurt. He went inside and stood at the front window to watch. Mr. Ybarra picked up the blue plastic cup from the driveway. He threw it in a big green trash bag on the tailgate of his old pickup. Both Mateo and Roberto offered their father some of their sharbets. Mr. Ybarra shook his head, went to the water hose, and washed the melted sweet treat from the driveway.

Mr. Ybarra never changed his expression or spoke during the ordeal. Neither had Joseph's father, other than to tell Joseph to go home. How could two grimy, wild, shirtless boys intimidate grown men into silence?

Joseph went to the kitchen, jerked the plastic liner out of the trash can, and carried the can to the backyard. The searing heat that troubled his belly worked upward. His hands trembled with rage. It only grew worse when he unrolled the garden hose. His eyes watered again, boiling over. Finally, he exploded. Joseph flung away the hose and picked up the plastic trash can. He slammed it against the concrete porch steps over and over. He slammed it until the plastic split into useless pieces.

When the blister in his belly no longer exceeded the degrees on the thermometer, Joseph kicked away the remnants of the trash can. He sat down on the steps. Why wouldn't Baba ever confront anyone? Why did he let cashiers and other synagogue members speak down to him? Was Baba a coward? Even Miss Eleanor would have waded right in there with a yard rake, a grammatically correct tongue lashing, and a threat to call the boys' parents.

The screen door opened, its metal spring closure groaning,

stretching until the tension spread the coils wide. Joseph felt the curious silence before Maman spoke. Plastic shards lay around the bottom of the porch steps. "Come inside, Youssef-jun. Come get some sharbet. You're too hot out there."

2
CONSTRUCTION HAT

"LaLa, have you ever seen Baba get mad?" asked Joseph.

"Don't use 'mad,' dear. Someone who's mad is crazy. Your daddy isn't crazy," answered Miss Eleanor.

Joseph tried again. "Okay, have you ever seen him angry?"

"Not that I can recall. Why?"

"I don't understand why he lets people insult him. He just stands there like they didn't."

LaLa didn't say anything for a while. She never wasted words.

"Joseph, do you remember the first time we met?" asked LaLa. She gripped a huge pair of pruning shears like she had a steer by the horns. The bright, yellow-flowered work dress and plastic garden shoes were her only uniform other than her daily 1950s-style collared navy or brown dress with one-inch matching heels. Thanks to a weekly visit to the beauty shop, her short hair remained suspiciously brunette and precisely permed. Her slightly plump, perfectly rectangular body shape had probably not changed since the fifties either.

Today the hydrangea hedges between their houses fell under her critical eye. Late-August rain gave the flowers a new birth of freedom long past the Fourth of July. LaLa insisted that her yard maintain the same neat appearance as the stately old home.

"Emmm . . . I think we met when I was in first grade?" said Joseph. He gathered an armful of branches and placed them in the ancient wheelbarrow.

"Don't use 'uh' and 'em,' dear," cautioned Miss Eleanor. "Start talking when you have something to say."

"We met when I was in first grade," Joseph said with a grin. He spent several weeks each summer with relatives in Be'er Sheva, Israel. The standard Israeli version of the American "uh . . ." was "em . . ." He picked up the habit, along with several satisfying curse words in both Hebrew and Arabic.

Maman pulled his ear when she heard him try out a new curse word. She'd not objected to "em . . ." so he still used it. He still used the curse words, too, but he was careful when he used them. If Maman told Baba, it might go beyond an ear pull. Baba occasionally cursed in Farsi, but Joseph was supposed to pretend he didn't hear or know what a *pedar sagg* was. Well, after yesterday evening, Baba knew he'd heard.

LaLa agreed with Joseph. "Yes, I do believe you were in first grade. We met right here at this fence," said LaLa.

When he was younger, Joseph couldn't pronounce "Eleanor," but he'd managed "LaLa." The nickname stuck well to a music teacher. Joseph hadn't used English as much as Farsi until kindergarten, and in first grade, it was still a challenge.

"Baba was teaching Maman how to drive," said Joseph, recalling the meeting day. "They left me on the front porch while they drove around the block. Baba told Maman he couldn't risk his only son's life. He said, 'Please, woman, I'm not Abraham. I can't sacrifice my only son!'"

LaLa laughed. "Your father was white as a sheet when she parked in the driveway. That's not easy for a man of his complexion."

"Maman still doesn't parallel park," mused Joseph. "She'll walk a quarter of a mile from a parking lot to avoid it."

"No shame in that," said LaLa. Another branch fell beneath her critical eye. "I saw a white construction hat bobbing along these hedges that day. At first I thought it was a telephone lineman, but I couldn't imagine one that short. I had to come see who it was."

"I was supposed to stay on the porch swing," said Joseph. "But you had the parlor window up. I could hear you playing a waltz on the piano. I came closer so I could hear, but I couldn't find an opening in the wire fence."

Miss Eleanor grunted when she whacked another branch. Joseph put it quickly in the wheelbarrow, hoping he wouldn't get ticks or spiders on him. Or ants. He brushed off his arms. Or chiggers. He rubbed his left ankle with his right sneaker.

Miss Eleanor said, "Yes, I saw that white construction hat. I said, 'Who's there?' Your sweet little face popped up on the other side of these blue hydrangeas. You had the friendliest smile. I could barely see your eyes for that big hard hat. 'I'm Joseph Nissan,' you said. 'I live here. And I like your song.'"

Joseph continued the story for her. "And you said, 'Well, that's the most pleasing greeting I've ever had the honor to receive.' You held out your hand and said, 'How do you do, Mr. Joseph? I'm Miss Eleanor. And I like your hat.'"

"That's exactly the way it was," said Miss Eleanor, nipping

a branch. "I told you, 'That's a mighty big hat for such a little boy. You must have big plans.' You said, 'I'm a enengeneer like my baba, Miss LaLa. I'll build a gate right here so I can come to your house.' You were pretty proud of your baba back then."

Joseph could see where this was going. "Yes, ma'am."

"Is there any reason you shouldn't still be proud to wear his hat?"

The word "coward" came to mind, but Joseph couldn't bring himself to say it out loud. He said, "He won't stand up for himself. Even when people are wrong."

"But are you still proud of your daddy?"

Joseph considered before he answered. "Yes, ma'am."

"Why?"

"He has a good job. He takes care of Maman and me. He's kind to everyone."

LaLa nodded. "Have you read *To Kill a Mockingbird*, Joseph?"

"Yes, ma'am. It was on my summer reading list for English." That was clever of her. He'd left the book at her house a few times. LaLa kept making him say yes. She was leading up to something.

"Were there things that Jem and Scout didn't know about their daddy? And Boo Radley?"

"Yes, ma'am."

What the heck did that mean? There were lots of things Joseph didn't know about his baba and Maman when they lived in Iran. Joseph was born in California. They'd moved to Texas after that. When his parents talked about Iran, it was about the food, the songs, the Jewish holidays, the cherry trees, and poetry.

Miss Eleanor dropped the shears to her side. She wiped the

sweat from her brow with a handkerchief. "Someday, Joseph, you'll appreciate how brave your daddy was. And then you'll appreciate how brave he is. Dear, wearing Mr. Kamran Nissan's hat is earned with a lot of suffering and bearing hard burdens."

"Yes, ma'am." No sense in ruining her winning streak of yeses.

Miss Eleanor said, "Today you're tall enough to step right over these hydrangeas. You play those waltzes better than any of my recital students. Time sure has changed how big these hedges look to you, hasn't it?"

LaLa was too smart. She was better at mind games than he was. And he was pretty good.

On that August day six years ago, he'd taken on LaLa as his personal responsibility. Joseph's next-door neighbor, babysitter, and piano teacher needed his daily supervision. Joseph had never met her deceased husband, Mr. Thaddeus, but he thought he could recognize him if his ghost decided to pop into LaLa's parlor and pick up the fiddle one day. LaLa had told Joseph all about him.

Mr. Thaddeus and LaLa had enjoyed nearly twenty-five years in the Forsling house before he passed away. LaLa said Mr. Thaddeus Forsling was a bookish man, happy with his accounting numbers by day and her company by night. The Forsling house had been built in 1917 by Mr. Thaddeus's father. It was a time when good Texas families built wide, hospitable porches and thick, solid doors.

Mr. Thaddeus had a talent to play the family's old fiddle. He loved playing "Yellow Rose of Texas," "Tennessee Waltz," and "Orange Blossom Special." LaLa and Mr. Thaddeus were childless. She taught music theory at the junior college until she retired. Now she gave piano lessons while the Forsling fiddle supervised from its mounting on the wall.

LaLa's students kept the rumor alive that the bowstrings would twitch if Miss Eleanor played a waltz. When Joseph asked her, LaLa said it was only a rumor. It had never kept Joseph from trying to make the bowstrings twitch with waltzes, though. Maybe he'd seen it once or twice. Your mind could play tricks on you in the old house.

LaLa said, "When your parents stepped out of the car that day we met, they both looked like they'd awakened from a terrible nightmare. Your baba was drenched in sweat. He'd soaked his handkerchief wiping his face. Your maman kept pulling wadded-up pink tissues from her purse for him. Little shreds of pink stuck all over his forehead and neck."

This made Joseph laugh. Maman always had a reserve of wadded-up tissues in her purse. That was his fault. When he was in first grade, he had enjoyed pulling the fresh, pink tissues from the package tucked in her purse, leaving her lots of unpackaged clean ones.

Joseph said, "When they got out of the car that day, Baba was mumbling to himself in Farsi. I tried to translate for you, and I told you that he was saying his head was dirty."

"Dirt on my head!" Miss Eleanor smiled at the memory. "A perfectly Persian way of saying he was as good as dead, but it didn't translate well. I tried my best to see where all that dirt was, but your father had as clean a full head of hair as I'd ever seen."

Joseph said, "Maman's still a nervous driver, but she's never wrecked. And I didn't stop pulling fresh tissues out of the packages in her purse until I was in second grade."

"How did she convince you to leave her purse alone?" asked Miss Eleanor.

Joseph said, "She put butterscotch candies in the side pocket and said I could look in only that pocket. If she caught me in the other part of her purse, then no candy. It cured me."

"Nothing works so well with second graders as a bribe," agreed LaLa. "That's how I get my Sunday school class to memorize their Bible verses. If Mr. Rehkopf's store ever gets rid of the Brach's candy bin, we'll lose the next generation of Southern Baptists."

Joseph felt eyes on him. He looked toward the street. Two shirtless boys sat on their bicycles, watching. The possum-faced boy who ruined Mr. Ybarra's fresh peach sharbet made a girlish pucker with his lips. "Pretty Boy," he called to Joseph, "you work the garden like a good Mexican." They laughed and rode away, each popping wheelies.

Joseph hated them. And he wasn't afraid of the police.

3

BLUE BONNET

"What's the latest?" asked Joseph. He imagined his cousin Shahla unkinking the phone cord in her kitchen in California. She was fifteen. It was their weekly Sunday-evening phone call. Long-distance rates were their lowest then. They always started their conversations by telling the funny things that happened when their parents misunderstood English. Usually it was their mothers who didn't speak English as well as their fathers.

"Hit the button," said Shahla, and she giggled.

"Oh, yeah," said Joseph. "That's a funny one. Your maman, right?"

Shahla giggled again. "Yeah. We were on the elevator, and this guy runs in as the door closes and says, 'Hit the eight button, please.'"

Joseph said, "So did you let her?"

"No," said Shahla. "I pushed the button for the eighth floor, and the elevator took us up to the sixth floor, and we got off. Maman looked at the man like he was crazy."

Her adopted maman. Shahla's real father was Joseph's uncle, his mother's older brother. Maman's brother and his wife, Shahla's mother, were killed in a terrorist car bomb in Israel when Shahla was only five years old. Shahla was safe because she was staying with her babysitters in Los Angeles. She had a grown older brother, but he'd disappeared after the bombing. Her babysitters adopted Shahla, but she still spent summers and holidays with Joseph.

"Did you explain it to her?" asked Joseph.

"Not until later. But it was so funny . . . when we got on the elevator to go down after the appointment, she stared real hard at the buttons like it was the first time she'd ever ridden an elevator, like maybe she'd missed something she was supposed to know about it. She finally took two fingers and punched the ground floor button really hard."

Joseph laughed. He could visualize Shahla's deep-green eyes twinkling. Her adopted parents were old, so she was gentle with them. Joseph would have tied them in knots within a week.

"What about you?" asked Shahla.

"Horseback riding," said Joseph.

"Huh?"

"I told Maman that I got my jeans so dirty because I was horseback riding with the twins at their ranch. I said it in English, and she looked at me like I got off the little cheese bus."

"What wasn't clear about horseback riding?" asked Shahla.

"Maman said, 'What other part of a horse would you ride on?'"

Shahla laughed softly.

Joseph said, "LaLa still laughs because Maman kept trying to figure out how I 'played by ear' on the piano. I knew Maman was staring at me pretty hard when she'd watch me play, but it took a while for her to come out and ask."

"Is Miss Eleanor coming to your bar mitzvah?" asked Shahla.

"Yeah. The twins are coming too," said Joseph.

"I like Mateo," said Shahla. "He's very courteous. I'm not sure why he hangs around with you."

"Thanks, Cousin," said Joseph. "I told Roberto that he better not come on to you. He thinks you're hot."

"Hot? Oh, yeah. That kind of hot."

"You're worse than our mothers," said Joseph. "And you can't blame that on Farsi."

"I don't hang around with nasty-mouth boys," said Shahla.

"And don't you forget it," said Joseph. "If any guy tries to touch you, I'll crush him."

Maman came into the kitchen. "Youssef-jun, let me say hello to Shahla. Your ten minutes is up. That's two dollars and ninety cents."

"Quick," said Joseph to Shahla. "What did I just think?"

Shahla was quick. "She spends more money than that every week on . . . emmm . . ."

"Shabbat flowers," said Joseph hurriedly. "Love you, Shahla-jun." He handed the phone to Maman. Maman talked for another five minutes. By Joseph's calculation, it was a dollar and forty-five cents more than their weekly long-distance limit. Tenderness came into Maman's voice, and a soft light crept into her eyes when she spoke to Shahla. It was the kind of happiness that you couldn't be jealous of. When his cousin came to visit, it was hard to pry her away from Maman. Joseph wanted to do more practical things with Shahla, like teach her to play basketball and ride a dirt bike. Maybe Shahla reminded Maman of her dead brother.

Joseph knew Maman wanted to adopt Shahla, but Baba

hadn't let her. Joseph wondered why. It would have brought Maman so much happiness. You didn't leave family behind without a pretty good reason. You didn't withhold happiness for no reason. Joseph wanted to know the reason.

4

FUNNY HAT

The wooden floor creaked, announcing Miss LaNell's entrance. Joseph tracked Miss LaNell's entry from the front door to LaLa's kitchen. He was in the restroom drying his hands. LaLa was in the kitchen, alerted by her sister's march across the wooden floor. "Eleanor Forsling," whispered LaNell, "is that little Arab boy with the funny cap here *again*?"

"Yes, sister," replied Eleanor. "And he's neither Arab nor little. They're Persian Jews, and he's growing like a weed."

Joseph was almost thirteen. Not a little boy. He opened the door quietly and inched down the short hallway.

"Where is he?" LaNell whispered loudly enough for Joseph to hear. When his parents whispered, he could never hear them. Texans did everything big and loud, even whispering.

LaLa opened a cabinet door and closed it back. She must have taken down a glass and poured her older sister a glass of sweet tea. "He's in the restroom. He knocked out half that pitcher of lemonade while my last student insulted Momma's piano by practicing a Chopin recital piece. I swear it sounded like she was typing an obituary on the keys. I can only hope that her parents have poor hearing. That Persian boy can play the entire piece by ear."

"It's not proper," objected LaNell. Joseph heard the *whoosh-squish* of the plastic cushion as she sat on a kitchen chair at the table. Joseph could visualize her keeping her purse in her lap as though the stray brown boy might dash in and snatch it at any moment. She always did that when he was around.

"It is proper," argued Eleanor. "He flushes and puts the seat down every time. And I hear the water running, so he washes his hands."

"No, I mean his coming over here every Saturday. Do you even charge him for lessons?"

"He doesn't come over every Saturday. His family stays in the city for religious services once or twice a month. And there's no reason to charge. He mows my lawn, changes my light bulbs, and takes out my trash. His mother sends over cookies for my students. His father fixed my screen door, repaired the carriage house roof, and took care of that big tree that fell over in the storm last year. I'm coming out on top, but I wouldn't charge anyway. He's a joy to teach." Joseph heard LaLa pour herself a glass of tea and *whoosh-squish* into a seat. "Put your purse down. He's not a thief."

"But the Jews killed our Lord and Savior Jesus Christ. They're cursed," said Miss LaNell.

"I'm not sure where your precious King James was printed, dear sister," said LaLa, "but mine says Jesus was a Jew, the Romans killed Christ, the Jews are beloved of God, and God will bless anyone who blesses them and curse anyone who curses them." Joseph could picture her pushing up her rimless octagon spectacles for effect. "Try to keep your good Southern Baptist curses straight."

Joseph smiled and eased through the door into the kitchen. He was clad in dress trousers and a sharply pressed white shirt. A blue kippah with a decorative silver border perched atop his black curls. "Good afternoon, Miss LaNell," he said politely. His Southern hospitality skills had been honed by Miss Eleanor. As far back as he could remember, LaLa spoke to him like an adult. She did that to all her piano students.

"Good afternoon, young man," Miss LaNell replied stiffly.

"Thank you for the lemonade, LaLa-jun," said Joseph. "I'd better get home."

"Tell your maman thank you for the cookies."

Miss LaNell spoke up. "Why isn't a strong young man like you playing outside on such a nice day?"

Joseph stopped in the doorway. "It's Shabbat. I have to go pray with my father." He turned and flashed the white-haired old woman a grin. "I'll pray that no one steals your purse."

Joseph didn't linger to enjoy her indignant gasp or LaLa's wide, wrinkled, red-lipstick smile. He walked toward the front door at a good clip.

Miss LaNell said to LaLa, "Of all the disrespectful . . ."

Joseph stopped at the piano and considered. Abruptly he pulled out the bench and sat.

The notes interrupted Miss LaNell's protest. She paused and turned her head. Joseph played a slow Texas rhythm. He sang: "'An orchid is a flower that blooms so tenderly . . .'" He glanced into the kitchen.

LaLa sipped her tea and watched her sister.

Joseph continued singing. It was the song that LaLa had said was wedged in her sister's heart like a ship that could never escape its moor inside a bottle. It reminded her of her first love who moved to Fort Worth to marry another girl. The song, LaLa said, could quiet Miss LaNell's heart and give her bittersweet solace. It was a reminder that some things simply must be accepted in pain and silence. Joseph continued passionately: "'I overlooked an orchid while searching for a rose . . .'"

Miss LaNell sat motionless until he finished. Quiet settled over the house, and Joseph returned to the doorway. He smiled, put his hand to his heart, and bowed slightly. "A beautiful song for a beautiful lady, Miss LaNell." With a bit of worry, he said, "Please don't tell Baba that I played on Shabbat, LaLa-jun." Joseph turned and walked toward the front door. Problem solved.

"Did you . . . ?" he heard Miss LaNell ask LaLa.

"Longest fingers I've ever seen on a twelve-year-old," interrupted LaLa. "He was born to play the piano, and he loves it. His father's never let him play in a recital. I wish his father didn't think it was a waste of time. Something tells me change is coming."

5
THINKING CAP

Joseph attended synagogue in Dallas on Saturdays for Shabbat with his family at least once per month and the Jewish holidays. His parents took a long nap on Shabbat afternoon. When they were in Dallas, Joseph was free to visit his synagogue friends. When the family remained in Hazel on Shabbat, they didn't mind if he went to LaLa's house. In fact, they were usually glad for Joseph to go somewhere else while they took that nap. Since Baba was gone for work so much, Joseph figured they caught up on their talking. He was pretty sure they weren't sleeping the whole time.

Joseph walked to LaLa's on Saturday afternoon with a plateful of almond cookies and Persian halvah candy. Only the cookies survived the walk between houses. Joseph amused himself on the long Shabbat afternoons by listening to LaLa's piano students plow through the classics. Joseph later imitated their mistakes and exaggerated them, which made LaLa laugh until she cried. Other times he'd play the Persian Jewish holiday melodies.

Joseph had never met his own grandparents. They either died in Iran years before he was born or still lived there, so Joseph adopted LaLa. This caused a few problems over the years when Jewish religious law crash-landed in Hazel, but Miss Eleanor was a Texas lady. Problems were not things to complain about. Problems were meant to be solved, like a sour key on her piano required a call to the piano tuner in Dallas.

This afternoon, LaLa's last student had finished her lesson, but her father had not picked her up. LaLa invited the student to continue practicing while she excused herself to hang a load of laundry. Joseph tiptoed to the doorway from the kitchen and listened. The girl was Vonda Baer. She was in Joseph's class one year in elementary school. He'd seen her in the hallway at the junior high school. He liked her honey-colored hair, her kind blue eyes, and light complexion. Her eyes were the color of the star and bars on the Israeli flag. Joseph's own eyes were *sabz*, green. Maman said no one could choose an eye color, but everyone could choose the light that shone through them.

The girl bungled a chord. When she glanced up in frustration, she saw Joseph. He smiled. She smiled back. "I'm glad Miss Eleanor went outside," Vonda said. "She does that funny thing with one side of her mouth when I mess up."

Joseph said, "That's Johann Pachelbel's 'Canon in D,' and it can be hard to play. Girls like that one."

"You can play it?" she queried.

"If you help me," Joseph offered.

"I'm afraid we're stuck then," she answered. "Didn't you hear me wreck it? I can't do it."

"Sure you can," assured Joseph. He walked to the bench and took a seat beside her. The girl didn't move away, so Joseph pressed closer, elbow to elbow. "Play it again," he instructed. After an interval, Joseph joined in, playing a harmonizing tune. When they reached the end, she started over. This time, Joseph added a honky-tonk ending, which made her giggle. LaLa had started doing that when he was a little kid to make him laugh.

"That was fun," she said, turning those two star-blue eyes toward him. "We made it sound like a real song instead of like trying to start a lawn mower over and over."

Joseph said, "Miss Eleanor will be pleased. Play your favorite song."

"It's not classical," the girl said. "It took me forever to work out the notes. I can't play it when my dad's in the house. He doesn't like rock and roll. He's a preacher."

"Play it anyway," urged Joseph.

She looked embarrassed, but she began to play "Don't Go Breaking My Heart." When she finished, he imitated it perfectly, only faster. She said, "You play it better."

"I play by ear, so it's easier for me. I've heard it on the radio. You know the words?"

She nodded.

"Okay, I'll play, and you sing."

"I don't know . . ."

Joseph played, and they sang a duet. "Want to do it faster?" he asked. She nodded, and they produced a faster version. When they finished, they laughed.

"Want some cookies?" asked Joseph.

"Sure," said Vonda.

Joseph stood and graciously beckoned. "They're in the kitchen." Vonda followed him, and Joseph pulled out a chair for her.

"Will you be in the fall recital?" asked Vonda.

Joseph shrugged and said, "I always set up the chairs." To get her mind off the recitals, he offered, "I'll pour you some lemonade." Joseph set two cookies for her on a saucer, and he poured her lemonade into a glass. For himself, he used a napkin and paper cup for his snack.

"Why are you using a paper cup?" asked Vonda. An entire shelf of clean glasses was in the cabinet.

"I . . . em . . . can't eat or drink from Miss Eleanor's dishes."

"Why not?"

"I'm Jewish," Joseph answered. "I mean, I'd probably break everything. I'm pretty clumsy."

Vonda considered. "I already know you're not clumsy. You can play the piano ten times better than me. What's 'Jewish'? Like in the Bible?"

"Uh . . . yeah. Like in the Bible." LaLa's Christian Bible was like his own in the front, but it was arranged differently, and there was an extra section that made it Christian. Joseph was an only child, and he didn't have much experience with girls. He needed a topic that they had in common. The Bible seemed safe.

"I always thought you were Mexican," said Vonda. "You have an accent."

"I have an accent?" Joseph asked.

"You do, but not bad. You put 'eh' in front of some words. Like, 'You want to do it eh-faster?' Is it a Jewish accent?"

"Not really. My parents speak Farsi. They're from Iran. Miss Eleanor helps me pronounce things better in English. She calls it 'elocution.'"

"Your parents are Pharisees?" asked Vonda.

"What's a Pharisee?" asked Joseph.

"You know, the hypocrites in the Bible," she said.

"I don't know what a Pharisee is," said Joseph. "I said they speak Farsi. Persian. It's a language in Iran."

"Where's Iran?"

"The Middle East."

"Where the Arabs live?"

"I'm not Arab!" Joseph slammed down the empty paper cup. He wasn't quite over the hypocrite thing.

"Gee, I'm sorry," Vonda apologized softly.

"It's . . ." Joseph struggled. Americans were an ocean away from his family culturally. Being Jewish complicated it. "We're Persian, not Arab. It's different."

"And that's why you can't eat off real plates?"

Joseph sighed. "I can eat off plates, but we can't eat from things that touch unkosher foods or mix meat and dairy foods. Miss Eleanor keeps paper plates and cups for me and a separate lemonade pitcher. Can't we talk about something else?"

"Is asking about your little cap 'something else'?"

"It's just a kippah. Try something else."

"Did you learn to play the piano from Miss Eleanor?"

"Yes. I live next door."

"You've heard a lot of bad piano playing then."

Joseph took her hand, examining the soft, white skin curiously. "You do fine." He set her warm hand down opposite his on the table. "Watch what I do, and then see if you can do it. It might help." She watched while he did a finger exercise like playing chords on the tabletop. "Now you try." He scooted his chair around so their hands were side by side to make it easier for her to imitate.

Suddenly, the kitchen door swung open. Reverend Baer

filled the doorway. With one look at Joseph, his face grew hard. "Where is Miss Eleanor?"

"She's hanging laundry," stammered Vonda.

"Who is this boy?" Reverend Baer demanded.

"He's . . . Joseph. He lives next door."

"Get in the car, Vonda."

Vonda hurried out without saying goodbye. Joseph was not sure why the man was upset.

Reverend Baer said, "Stay away from my daughter, Jewish Boy. 'What fellowship hath Christ with Belial? or what part hath he that believeth with an infidel?' The blood of Christ is on your head, son. Repent, be washed in Jesus's blood, and remove the curse from your head." The man turned and left.

Joseph wondered why the man thought there was blood on his kippah. And how could even more blood help? Every Shabbat before the meal, Joseph and Baba put on their kippahs. His father pressed his large hands firmly upon Joseph's head, whispering blessings and endearments. Those warm hands clasped Joseph's cheeks while he kissed them, hugging him close. Joseph breathed in the scents of heavy starch in Baba's dress shirt and the clove of his Shabbat shower. "Youssef-jun," Baba whispered, "nooré cheshm-am." *Joseph-dear, you are my life and the light of my eyes.* Baba's weekly blessing was the highlight of Joseph's week.

Christians were a puzzle. If they were like LaLa, the Ybarras, and Vonda, they were good-hearted, sensible, friendly people. If they were like this man, they were angry people obsessed with blood. Maybe the man was exaggerating. Farsi was a language full of strange expressions. Maybe preachers had their own.

Joseph unclipped his kippah and turned it in his hands. Could a little kippah cause this kind of trouble?

That evening the phone rang. Baba answered. From his room, Joseph followed the conversation with Reverend Baer. His heart sank. He longed to hear Baba defend him, but Baba agreed with the blood-obsessed reverend.

"Yes."

"Yes."

"No."

"He touched her?"

"I agree."

"No, is not permitted."

"No, we do not permit."

"I am sorry. I will speak to him immediately."

"Yes, I will see to it. He will understand. I regret."

"Sorry there is problem, but no more mistake."

"Yes, thank you. Goodbye."

The phone clacked down into its cradle. Joseph realized he was holding his breath. He heard Baba walk down the hall and stop at his door. He then opened it. Baba sat on the bed beside him. "You're spending too much time at Miss Eleanor's. An hour or so at her house is enough."

"But LaLa needs me, Baba. I promised her I'd set up the chairs for the recital . . ."

Baba brushed aside Joseph's protest. "Time to grow up, Youssef. No more coddling by your maman and Miss Eleanor. You're taking on the obligations of a Jewish man at your bar mitzvah soon. You've violated Shabbat by playing the piano. You touched a girl. This will not happen again, you understand?" Baba stood, gently pinched Joseph's ear, and left him alone. He didn't wait for Joseph to say yes. It probably never occurred to Baba that Joseph would defy him.

6
BASEBALL CAP

"What's the latest?" asked Shahla.

"School shopping," said Joseph. "We were doing okay up until sneakers, tennis shoes, and dress shoes."

"Oh, yeah," said Shahla. "That's a red zone."

"Are you unkinking the phone cord?" asked Joseph.

The hesitation on the other end told Joseph he was right.

"No," Shahla said.

"That's because you just stopped," said Joseph.

"But I'm not doing it now."

Joseph grinned and said, "Maman and I went to the shoe store at the mall. The salesman was this tired old bird, you know, probably just lost his job selling vacuum cleaners. I thought it would scare him if the brown people spoke Farsi, so I told Maman in English that I needed sneakers for school."

"Problem?" asked Shahla.

"Maman says, 'Youssef-jun, why you need for to sneak at de school? You don' go eh-sneakin' 'round de school. You get in

de trouble, and I have to call to your baba at work.' The salesman looked at us like . . ."

"I can imagine," said Shahla.

"And then," Joseph continued. "I told her I needed white
tennis shoes. You know, for gym class. She was already on a roll,
and she says, 'De Shah of Iran de only Persian in de worl' who
play tennis, Youssef. Why you need dis tennis shoe?'"

Shahla laughed aloud. "That's pretty funny," Shahla said.
"You gotta admit, that's funny."

"The salesman wasn't amused. When he heard me tell her
that Baba said to get black dress shoes to go with my bar mitzvah suit, he rolled his eyes practically back in his head."

"Emmm . . . do I dare ask what she said?" asked Shahla.

"She said, 'Youssef, you don' making any sense today. Nex'
time I send you wit' your fader to buy de shoe. Boy don' wear
dress to bar mitzvah whedder dey black or any odder color.'"

Shahla gave a rare belly laugh. "Now *that* I'd like to see. You
in a black dress at your bar mitzvah."

Joseph said, "I'm pretty sure the salesman went back to the
vacuum cleaner store."

"Oh, my baba finally got you a Houston Astros cap," said
Shahla. "I'll bring it to your bar mitzvah."

"Wow, thanks!" said Joseph. Shahla's adopted baba sold to
major sports stadiums, supplying them roasted nuts for conces-
sions. He often received free tickets to baseball games, reserved
seats at the racetrack, and souvenir hats. With Shahla's prompt-
ing, he'd obtained Joseph a collection of ballcaps and tickets to a
Rangers game. Joseph had the prized Dallas Cowboys and Texas
Rangers caps. The Houston Astros had been elusive.

Shahla said, "I had to apply a little pressure. I hinted that if

Baba didn't want Maman to find out that he checks me out of school to go to the horse races sometimes, and that I can read a Daily Racing Form and bet the exacta and trifecta, then it would be nice to have an Astros cap. He got me a signed one."

Joseph had to laugh. Shahla was quiet, but she was clever when she really wanted something.

"In fact," said Shahla, "he was so motivated that he got three signed hats, so you can give one to Mateo and Roberto."

"Who signed them?" asked Joseph.

"César Cedeño."

"Are you kidding me?"

"Why?" asked Shahla. "Is he famous or something?"

"Or something," said Joseph. "Please tell your baba that I'll be his servant for life, and I'm not worthy of his generosity, I dance circles around him, and any other *taarof* thing that pops into your head."

"Youssef-jun," called Maman from the living room.

Joseph had to hurry. "Hey, I met this girl . . ."

Maman's steps approached the kitchen.

"Anyway, later," said Joseph.

"What am I thinking?" asked Shahla.

"Why do I leave you hanging when I know I have to hang up," said Joseph, and he handed the receiver off to Maman.

7
WATCH CAP

The beginning of the school year was exciting. Now that he was in eighth grade, Joseph took seven classes per day. The hallway was a great place to be admired. With Joseph's coaching, Maman had purchased the cool-kid, basic male uniform of Levi's 501s, V-neck shirts with stripes from collar to sleeves, and striped sneakers.

Some of the kids, the "goat ropers," wore Levi's, Justin boots, and cowboy-style shirts. Other kids wore jeans and T-shirts promoting rock concerts they were too young to attend. University of Texas, Dallas Cowboys, and Texas A&M logos were acceptable formal or casual wear for anyone. Smaller groups liked to call themselves gangs. You could blame the English teachers for that. They'd assigned *The Outsiders* for class reading in seventh grade. After that, little groups such as the Posse Comitatus popped up.

In the wintertime, the Posse liked to wear long, cowboy-style dusters, but they'd melt like a chocolate bar in a hot car in this late-summer heat. The Posse could have picked a more practical uniform. Anyone could pick out the D&D's, Delinquents and Druggies, from the smell of cigarettes, no special clothes required. In junior high, everyone had to fit somewhere.

Because he was in the advanced math and science classes, Joseph hung out with the smart kids sometimes, but lunch determined your social group. Joseph had eaten with the Hispanics since kindergarten.

Thursdays were "Pep Day," and almost everyone wore some form of the school hawk logo. Texans were serious about football. The gym filled on Thursday afternoons for the pep rally. The cheerleaders led the cheers and skits; the band played the school fight song. The football players sat together in chairs on the gym floor in their Levi's and football jerseys.

The coaches tried to look interested. The vice principals marched in late with the kids who sneaked a smoke in the bathroom. The teachers played whack-a-mole with gum chewers, paper-ball throwers, and the gravest of sinners, those who didn't sit in their assigned bleacher area with homeroom. Joseph liked stomping his feet on the wooden bleachers while the cheerleaders whipped everyone into a frenzy: "Beat 'em, bust 'em, that's our custom, go, Hawks, go!" The noise was thunderous. Sometimes one of the varsity players juked or pumped his fist, which lifted the noise level from thunderous to ear-splitting. Joseph liked school. A lot. It was one place he fit in.

Since Joseph had touched Vonda Baer, something about the girls at the pep rallies excited him more. He noticed the cheerleaders' long, bare legs when they did cartwheels. The cheerleaders were like grown women with fully formed bodies, perfect makeup, big loopy earrings, and confidence.

This Thursday, the varsity was playing its first away game. That meant white visitor jerseys with black-and-gold numbers and sleeve stripes. The players stood with four fingers jammed into their pockets, feet square, looking smug. Joseph noticed the two boys who had ruined the peach sharbet standing among the football players. One of them stood on the first row, which meant he was a starter. The other one stood on the third row, which meant he wasn't. Well, that could ruin a pep rally. Thugs.

Joseph climbed the wooden bleachers to the stomping chant, "'We will . . . we will . . . rock you.'" He pushed his way to Mr. Chappelle's homeroom section and sat at the end of a row. Amid the waving pom-poms and spirit rags, Joseph turned and scanned the bleachers. His two homeroom buddies hadn't made it yet, so he scooted over and left a little space on the end of the row. When Roberto and Alex started up the bleachers, Joseph stood and waved his hand so they'd see him. They both carried English textbooks. They'd probably gotten out of class late and decided to carry them rather than stop to put them in their lockers.

On the gym floor below, the possum-faced football player in the third row caught Joseph's eye. He mouthed, "Pretty Boy," and blew Joseph a kiss.

"*Pedar sagg*," Joseph shouted back.

The boy made a vile motion with his hand and forearm. It was so fast that none of the teachers or coaches saw it.

"*Ahbal*," added Joseph.

"Who you calling a dumbass?" asked Roberto. They exchanged curse word vocabulary. Roberto could curse in Farsi almost as well as Joseph could curse in Spanish.

Joseph pointed down to the third row on the gym floor.

"Yeah," said Roberto. "*Tonto*."

Joseph was no longer interested in the peach thug, though. He'd spotted Vonda Baer two rows down and to his left. Her honey-colored hair was styled back in deep feathers, dripping blonde layers down her back. There was a narrow aisle between the two sections, and a little space to the right of her. Joseph glanced over at Mr. Chappelle, who probably would give anything to be in the teacher's lounge with a cigarette and a Styrofoam cup of burnt coffee. A peppermint lozenge didn't cover up those smells.

"Give me your English book," said Joseph to Roberto.

"What for? You gonna carry my books to class for me?" Roberto joked.

"Nah. Hers." Joseph grabbed Roberto's book and gently tossed it underhand. It tumbled into the foot space of Vonda's row. She looked over her shoulder.

Joseph tiptoed down the narrow strip of bleachers until he reached her row. "Hey," he said, and reached down for the English book. "Sorry. Lost my grip."

Vonda smiled at him. She was wearing a Hawks spirit shirt, jeans, and a puka-shell necklace with matching earrings. Star-blue eyes, each star a glittering, miniature smile. Joseph felt like he was going to fall down the bleachers.

Just then, the band started playing the national anthem. Joseph straightened and put his hand over his heart to sing along. Vonda smiled and leaned closer to hear him, so he sang a little louder. The school song followed, and Joseph risked a look over his shoulder. Mr. Chappelle glared at him. Joseph held up the book and made an apologetic expression. By then, the empty spaces between the sections were packed with standing students.

It would be almost impossible to get back to his assigned home-room section. Mr. Chappelle glared harder but shook his head. Joseph was to stay put.

For forty-five minutes, Joseph was only barely aware of the activities on the floor below. He'd always envied the football players, but he wouldn't trade places with any of them today, especially the one who kept scowling at him from the third row.

8
MAD HATTER

Joseph sat on the curb of Rehkopf's Grocery with a paper bag. He waited for LaLa to return with the forgotten baking soda. Baba would scold him if he knew that Joseph had carried the bag of groceries for LaLa. Groceries were *muktzeh*, a forbidden burden on Shabbat. Being Jewish on Saturday in Texas was a source of constant technical questions. He sighed, roasting in his dress shirt.

Two boys rode up on bicycles and leaned them against the brick wall of the store. They argued over what they would buy with their pooled resources of seventy-eight cents before they took notice of Joseph. Joseph didn't turn, hoping they wouldn't recognize him. No such luck. "Hey, kid," said one of them.

"Hey," said Joseph.

"What's that little doily on your head?"

Joseph could kick himself for not hiding his kippah in his pocket. It was a new one he'd received for his upcoming bar mitzvah. Plain black, like Baba's. "Nothing," he said.

The other boy sneered. "Why does it have a girl's hair clip in it? Are you queer or something?"

Joseph knew what queer was, but there was something in the way the boy said it. Maybe it didn't mean exactly what Joseph thought it did. He looked around, and the grime on the first boy's sneakers matched the grime on the school mascot ballcap. The cap proclaimed: "Fighting Hawks." It wasn't very respectful of the school bird to let the cap get so dirty. Dirty birds.

"He's a homo," pronounced the first boy. "Look at that girly face and those sissy clothes. Hey . . . you're the Mexican kid that hollered at me."

Joseph remained silent, wishing he didn't have long eyelashes and rosy cheeks that earned affectionate pinches from Maman and his aunts. They exclaimed, *"Moosh bokhoradet!"* when they pinched his cheeks. It was a good thing that his synagogue friends didn't know that it was Farsi for "A mouse should eat you!" He'd end up being called Moosh for the rest of his life.

"Whatcha got in this bag?" the grimy boy asked. He rummaged through the paper sack beside Joseph. The boy grunted in disgust and flung a can of Eagle Brand milk at Joseph. The unexpected missile bounced off Joseph's arm. Ouch. The boy had good aim.

Joseph started to protest, but the other boy moved behind him and swatted at his kippah, causing it to sit askew. "Got any change?" the boy asked. "With clothes that fancy, you're packin' some money. Let's have it."

"I don't carry money on Shab . . ." Joseph stopped. They didn't have any idea what Shabbat was, so they wouldn't understand why he wouldn't carry any money.

The boy smacked the back of his head again. This time the kippah fell to the curb. "Out with it, sissy wetback," he ordered.

"I'm not . . ." Again, Joseph halted. Was being Persian any better than being Mexican or whatever else they were calling him?

"Retard," said the grimy boy. "Can't even finish a sentence." He withdrew the carton of eggs and threw them one by one at the brick wall of the store. The eggs ran down the building and pooled on the hot concrete. It created floating islands of broken shells. The boy aimed the last one at Joseph.

Joseph stood and dodged the egg, although it would have hurt less than the Eagle Brand. The boy standing behind him pushed him, but Joseph didn't fall. His father had taken him to boxing lessons since he was in third grade. His balance was good. Joseph turned to face his tormentors. The grimy boy with the catlike eyes threw a stick of margarine at him. Joseph batted it away. Three more sticks followed rapidly. The last one hit Joseph in the face.

Joseph surveyed the broken eggs and sticks of margarine melting and cooking on the sidewalk skillet of Texas heat. He walked to where the Eagle Brand rolled to a stop, and he stooped and retrieved it. Elsie the Cow beamed at him from the label.

Grimy Boy pulled out the last item from the paper bag, a bar of Baker's Chocolate. He peeled the wrapper and took a bite, but he spat it out, threw it aside, and spat twice more. "What the hell is that?" he asked Joseph. "It sure ain't chocolate."

"Cat's still got his tongue," answered the second boy, the one whose face reminded Joseph of a possum. He said, "Gimme your money, or I'll kick your ass like the stinking donkey you ride."

The thermometer in Joseph's belly spun. These thugs had ruined the ingredients of the cake LaLa was making for her

Sunday school class. They'd ruined Maman's peach sharbet. They'd ruined the paint job on Mr. Ybarra's truck. Joseph's long, slender fingers curled tightly around the can of sweet milk. "I'm not giving you any money," Joseph snarled. "I'm taking it. Give me every penny of that change."

The two boys laughed. "Or what?" smirked Grimy Boy. Joseph lunged and threw a punch loaded with the can of Eagle Brand. It grazed the boy's chin with a good thwack, knocking off his dirty cap. The other boy, who was smaller, grabbed Joseph, and they struggled. Meanwhile, Grimy Boy recovered and pummeled Joseph.

Joseph pulled away and timed a perfect punch to Possum Boy's nose, producing a blood fountain. Together, the boys pulled Joseph to the concrete. It was a punching, wrestling tangle. Drops of blood mingled with lakes of broken eggs.

"Joseph, stop! Stop it, I say!" ordered LaLa.

Joseph ignored her. To stop meant certain defeat, but he wasn't strong enough to finish it. His rage had consumed his energy. His arms felt leaden. Exhaustion crept in. Boxing was no help when the opponent refused to wait politely for you to get back to your feet and reset.

A huge push broom rained blows. Joseph and the cat-eyed grimy boy scrambled up. Mr. Rehkopf pounded all three of them. Grimy Boy finally got traction, and he ran toward his neighborhood. He may not have worried too much about Mr. Ybarra's edger, but he had a healthy respect for Mr. Rehkopf's broom.

LaLa was livid. "Joseph Nissan, what has gotten into you?"

Mr. Rehkopf paused with the broom, but Joseph ignored him. He walked to the two bicycles. He pulled a bicycle away from the wall, lifted it high, and slammed it sideways on the edge of the curb, leaving it wrecked. The front wheel came loose and bounced once before it gave a half roll and fell.

Joseph turned and glared at Mr. Rehkopf.

"Joseph Nissan, you go home this very instant. If you're not home by the time I get there . . ." LaLa threatened.

Joseph looked at LaLa. His confidence wavered. Pain bloomed everywhere. His shirt hung torn outside his pants. His nose bled, and both elbows were skinned and bleeding.

"G'wan, git like Miss Eleanor told you," Mr. Rehkopf barked, shaking the broom like LaLa when she broke up cats fighting on her back porch.

The possum kid made it to his feet, holding his split lip and bloody nose. "You, too," Mr. Rehkopf told him. He swatted the boy's rear end. The boy grabbed the remaining bicycle and pedaled off. "Well?" Mr. Rehkopf asked Joseph.

Joseph picked up his kippah and the can of Eagle Brand. He glanced at LaLa. "Sorry about the groceries," he said simply. He dropped the dented Eagle Brand into the empty sack, stuffed the kippah into a back pocket, and picked up the store receipt. Squinting through the throbbing, swimming haze of his swollen eye, Joseph walked home.

The receipt said six dollars and two cents for the groceries, including tax. He pocketed the receipt. It was *muktzeh* to carry a receipt on Shabbat, but what was one more sin? There was a lot to think about. What was a homo or a queer? Did wearing your best clothes make you a homo or queer, or was it the kippah? Was a homo a Hispanic?

Until now, discipline hadn't been very frightening. Baba never went beyond a swat on the rear end or an ear pull. Even if Joseph hadn't gone inside the store, just walking to a store, carrying the groceries, and fighting on Shabbat was an overwhelming list of offenses. Maybe Baba would accept that he'd walked LaLa to the store to keep her safe. With Baba, taking care of widows and the elderly was very important. Maybe.

9

PASS THE HAT

Baba sat in his recliner reading. Maman was setting the table for the last meal of Shabbat. Both looked up when Joseph came through the front door. There was shocked silence. Maman asked, "What happened, Youssef? Are you hurt?"

"I was in a fight . . . at the grocery store."

This brought a different kind of silence. They examined Joseph, noting the dried blood, scratches, and swollen eye. Baba took Joseph's kippah from his back pocket and clapped it roughly atop his mussed curls. "Go wash your face and hands, and then come eat. After *havdalah*, stay in your room while I make prayers."

It was the greatest shame. Joseph should be making prayers with Baba. He was supposed to be preparing for his bar mitzvah.

Joseph had no appetite. He wasn't sure whether his queasy stomach was the aftereffect of the fight or dread of Baba's displeasure. Aggressiveness was off-limits when it involved outsiders. His father had a terrible fear of the police. When Joseph declined to eat, Baba sent him to his room with a token morsel of bread.

Later, Maman brought him a cold glass of *doogh*, heavy on the mint for his stomach, which he gratefully accepted. She smoothed his curls around his ears and whispered words of comfort while he drank. Joseph wasn't sorry for fighting, but his heart ached at Maman's distress.

Baba appeared in the doorway and angrily beckoned her out of the room. *Yeah*, thought Joseph. *This time it will be bad.*

Joseph heard the knock on the front door that he knew was LaLa. Guilt overwhelmed him for losing her money. How many Chopin lawn mowers and how much Bach typewriting had LaLa suffered through to earn enough money for the ingredients? A few minutes later, the front door closed. The house grew silent.

Later Joseph heard his parents singing "Eliyahu HaNavi" without much conviction that Elijah the Prophet would ever show up. Within moments, he heard Baba praying the evening prayers in his study. Before he knew it, Baba was standing inside his bedroom door. Closing it.

"Strip," ordered Baba. Baba was tall. Joseph was proud that he also would be tall, but tonight he was afraid to look up. Joseph rolled off his bed and removed his bloody shirt, under-shirt, socks, and trousers. Baba motioned him to turn. In the heavy stillness, Joseph felt Baba's eyes repeating the examination on his backside.

"Lay across the bed, Youssef," Baba said. Joseph could hear the slight tinkle of the belt buckle and the slow slide of leather across fabric. Baba removed Joseph's kippah from his head and placed it on the nightstand. Out of the corner of his eye, Joseph saw Baba's big hand place his own black kippah beside Joseph's.

"Baba-jun . . ." tried Joseph. Surely his father wanted to hear what happened first, but a hand pushed him roughly across the bed. The blows fell on his backside until Joseph wept. The skin under his underwear felt aflame. When he could endure no more, Joseph turned to shield himself with a hand. He cried out brokenly, "Baba, *ozr mikhaam.*" *Daddy, I'm sorry.*

Baba stopped. Through soggy eyelashes, Joseph could see his father's face was also completely awash in tears. Baba's voice shook. "Youssef, you will control your rage. As long as you live in this house, you will protect Shabbat and this family. It's your duty as a Jew. You will not lead the authorities to our door."

"But Baba, you take me to boxing lessons. Why did you want me to learn how to fight when you won't let me fight?"

A deeper shadow of pain crossed Baba's face. He let the loop drop from the belt. "Self-defense was something that no Jew in a Middle Eastern country was permitted. We're in America, and I never know . . ."

Joseph waited, but Baba didn't finish. He curled the belt and set it on the nightstand. Baba said, "You are a cunning boy, Youssef. People will always hate us, but you can talk your way out of trouble." He motioned to Joseph to sit on the bed. Joseph sniffled in humiliation at having to beg for mercy.

"Youssef, fighting is a last resort. The school skipped you a grade because you are smart. Learn to make friends of your enemies."

"They didn't want to be friends, Baba," Joseph protested. Embarrassingly, his voice was so thin from emotion and pain that the words nearly evaporated as they left his lips.

"Youssef, do you know how many times I've been called a 'raghead,' a 'sand nigger,' and a 'camel jockey' by the people I work with?" asked Baba. "And that's before they find out I'm Jewish or start making fun of my accent."

Joseph shook his head, and Baba sat beside him.

"I was called a *jahud* in Iran by ignorant men who could barely add and subtract, much less design high-technology field instruments like I did. I worked for the National Iranian Oil Company, and some men wouldn't even take a blueprint from my hand. I was a *najis jahud*. I had to set it on the table first."

Joseph knew a *jahud* was Arabic for a Jew. "What's *najis*?" he asked.

Baba looked away. "It's ritually unfit and unholy, but not exactly. 'Filthy Jew.' There's no real English word for it. A language is part of its culture and religion. American culture does not need a word for this in English. They have hate words of their own. To me, it's just a religious word to put a pretty mask on hate."

"Why didn't we move to Israel with the rest of our family, Baba? They don't hate Jews in Israel."

Baba wiped the moisture from his face with a handkerchief. "They do hate some Jews in Israel, but you're too young to understand. I'm an oil field engineer. There are no oil jobs in Israel. What Arab corporation would hire a *jahud*? A Jew can't even live in Saudi Arabia."

"Is that why we moved here from California?"

"Yes, I needed work. Make friends, Youssef. You know how because you have lots of Hispanic friends. You try to use their language, which is respectful. You don't belittle them. Do the same with everyone. We had Muslim friends in Iran. We respected one another. Find the good people. No matter where you are, there are always a few." Baba handed Joseph a tissue from his nightstand. Joseph wiped his nose, which ran a thin mixture of snot and blood.

"The Mexicans are nice to me, Baba. I don't want to be nice to people who aren't nice to me."

Baba said, "I'm a good engineer, Youssef. That's what Americans respect, quality work that solves problems. They make more money in the oil fields when I solve problems. When I make them more money, I make more money. I concentrate on doing a better job than anyone else. That makes me friends even of my enemies."

"I don't have any money, Baba," objected Joseph. "What can I do better than anyone else?"

"You have to figure that out, *Aziz-am*. You're good at math already."

Baba had used a term of endearment, *Aziz-am*. His mood was softening. Joseph considered. On Shabbat afternoons, Baba and Joseph solved math problems as a game. Since it was forbidden to write on Shabbat, Joseph worked the sums mentally. Baba increased their difficulty. Because of it, he skipped a grade in elementary school. Now, Joseph was in an algebra class for advanced students.

It was odd for a skinny twelve-year-old to be in a math class for thirteen- and fourteen-year-olds, but extracurricular sports required passing grades. The eighth-grade athletes adopted him as their mascot who supplied homework answers. Other students regarded him with awe when the football players greeted him in the hallway. A varsity football jersey was a Hollywood star in Texas.

Baba placed his arm around Joseph's shoulder. Joseph winced. Baba asked, "Can you solve this?"

"I'll try."

Baba leaned over to check Joseph's shoulder. A nasty bruise

marked where the milk can had hit it. His father remained expressionless, resentment silenced by years of silent rage as a *dhimmi*. As a non-Muslim living in Muslim lands, Baba was granted safety in return for paying a special tax. But Jews never complained . . . Baba had told him once that where he grew up, no Jew would dare speak his mind or bring a case to court. "Violence is the last resort, Youssef," said Baba.

"Okay, Baba. I'll be the eagle."

"What?"

"The canned milk. The label says 'Eagle,' but there's a smiling cow on it. People will think I'm smiling, but I'm not inside. I'm just flying above their insults."

Baba said, "That's smart. And no more afternoons at Miss Eleanor's. No son of mine is going to be a *motreb*. Entertainment is not a decent Persian occupation. No more piano."

"But LaLa needs me . . ."

Baba brushed aside Joseph's protest. "Time to grow up, Youssef-jun. You have responsibilities. I love you." Baba stood, gently pinched Joseph's ear, and closed the door. Joseph was left alone to figure out how to outsmart two angry football players.

10
TOP HAT

The next Monday in gym class calisthenics, Joseph saw the coach assess his black eye, bruised arm, and skinned elbows and knees. Although the fear seemed silly, Joseph hoped that the coach's long look wouldn't involve the police somehow.

Coach Meeks lined up the boys for dodgeball in the gym. As the game progressed, Joseph gained accuracy and strength. He easily caught the hardest throws in his direction. He hunted the best players to pick off first. The exercise worked off his soreness.

An assistant coach emerged from the gym office. Together, he and Coach Meeks watched Joseph draw a bead on the last survivor. Joseph could see them watching him and talking. He moved down the painted line toward them, stalking his opponent.

"I can't remember what nationality the Nissan boy is, but he teams up with the Mexican kids for sports," said Coach Meeks to the other.

"He has an accent. Not much of one."

"I'd love to see him use that arm to throw a football," said Coach Meeks.

The assistant mused, "I've tried to recruit foreign kids before, and it didn't go well. Immigrant families include their children in family work and activities. It's the other way around here. Americans orbit around their kids' activities."

"Even so . . ." said Coach Meeks. "Don't you see that?"

Joseph threw hard, and the ball hit his last opponent on the ankle.

"Hit the showers, boys," instructed Coach Meeks. Joseph's teammates congratulated him. A black eye was a badge of honor, and Joseph's dodgeball win lent him renewed star status. His admirers couldn't know was what behind Joseph's smile. Rage. Control. Throw. Peach sharbet. Rage. Control. Throw. Blue Bonnet margarine. Rage. Control. Throw. Lucerne grade A large eggs. Rage. Control. Throw. Baker's Chocolate. Rage. Control. Throw. Eagle Brand milk. Rage. Control. Throw. Blue-eyed "Canon in D."

Coach Meeks called to Joseph, "Nissan, yo. Front and center."

Joseph stopped and turned. *Yo front and center?* Yo front and center of what?

Coach pointed to the hardwood in front of him. "That means here, son. Now."

When Joseph faced him, he was the same height. That was just too darn cool. He wondered if Shahla knew what "yo front and center" meant, or if it was a Texas phrase like "okey dokey." Joseph knew a lot of words because he'd always had to translate for Maman when Baba was working, but Texans never ran out of new words.

"Nissan, have you ever played football?"

"No, sir. Just basketball."

"Ever play a contact sport? You like to hit hard?"

"Boxing, sir. Yes."

"Never threw a football?"

"No, sir."

"Want to learn?" The coach removed his ballcap to rub a forearm across his balding head. He readjusted the cap, straightening the hawk emblem.

Joseph glanced at the cap. A slow smile spread across his face. "Yes, sir."

"Come to football practice after school today. Wear your gym clothes. Be on the field by 3:45 p.m."

"Yes, sir . . . but Coach, can I tackle, too?"

"If you're any good, we'll get you some equipment and a physical. We'll teach you all of it. Once you put on a helmet, you can tackle the whole team if you want to. Now go get showered."

"Yes, sir."

Permission to tackle? Yo front and center. Okey dokey.

11

PAPER HAT

Joseph rode his bike home from football practice, thinking of ways to present this new activity to his parents. Baba was away from home working. He wouldn't be back until Thursday night. Sometimes he was gone for three weeks at a time visiting oil fields. During those weeks, Joseph and Maman stayed home on Shabbat. She refused to drive all the way to Dallas, which might require parallel parking.

They kept their tiny rented garage apartment from when they lived in Dallas. It was within walking distance of the Dallas synagogue, but the owner required them to park on the curb, which was crowded on weekends. There was no way Maman would parallel park. Although she could read English, Maman made Joseph translate every single road sign on the interstate from English to Farsi. He had no idea how to translate the importance of Texas football to her.

One look inside the back-door window, and Joseph saw Maman was worried sick. Football practice had made him an hour and a half late. He was still in his grass-stained gym clothes. LaLa was there, and her ancient address book lay open on the table near the phone. She might have the numbers of Sam Houston and Stephen F. Austin if one looked under "H" and "A." Joseph took a deep breath and opened the back door. Yo front and center.

"Youssef, where have you been!" Maman said. It was an accusation, not a question. LaLa left her rimless octagon glasses perched far down her nose so that she could peer over them disapprovingly. The low-nose perch was always a bad sign. Singing a soothing song wasn't going to help him with these two ladies.

"The coach asked me to come to football practice after school," said Joseph. He spoke as rationally as possible, imitating Baba's serious tone.

"The school should have called if they were keeping you late," interjected LaLa.

"It wasn't planned," said Joseph. "I did really well in gym class today, and Coach asked me to stay over." He set down a sheaf of papers on the table and kissed Maman's cheeks. "Love you, Maman."

"Youssef . . ."

Joseph kept talking. "I need to go to a doctor for a physical, and you need to sign these papers so that I can play."

Maman didn't even look at the thick stack of English rules, disclosures, and forms. "And there's an equipment fee." Both women still stared at him. "And I need you to take me to the sporting goods store to get me a . . ." Here he faltered. Baba would be the best one to take him for a new athletic cup. ". . . custom mouthpiece," Joseph finished. He no longer felt comfortable having conversations with his mother that involved his *dhoul*. Certainly not in front of Miss Eleanor.

LaLa closed her address book and rose to leave. This was a family problem. "Can you at least sign the permission slip?" Joseph asked Maman. "So that I can keep working out until I get my physical? I'm not allowed to have contact, but I can do the conditioning drills and practice running routes and catching."

Maman looked at him helplessly, understanding none of what he said except that he needed the permission slip. She wasn't over the fact that he'd been missing for an hour and a half.

"Look, Maman-jun . . ." Joseph stopped, and LaLa looked up at him. His voice had cracked strangely. "Emmm . . ." LaLa's eyebrow raised in correction. Joseph tried again. "Maman . . ." This time his voice cooperated, ". . . Baba said I need to grow up and do more things that men do. This is something he'd want me to do. I just need you to sign the permission slip. I'll talk to him when he gets home."

LaLa gave him that look that said she knew he was manipulating his mother. It was only a slight movement of the right side of her mouth and right cheek, but Joseph knew the look. LaLa turned to leave.

Maman thanked Miss Eleanor for coming and calling around to locate Joseph, but Joseph was relieved when the front door closed behind LaLa. She always saw through the games he played. It took Joseph three hours of working on Maman that night before she finally put her signature on the permission slip.

————

Baba took the news better than Joseph thought he would. He looked through all the paperwork carefully. When Baba put down the papers, he told Maman, "He's trying to put a hat on your head."

"Trying to put a hat on your head" was a Persian way of saying you're trying to trick someone. Joseph felt the disappointment of yet another door slamming in his face. No, you can't because it's Shabbat. No, you can't because you're Jewish. No, you can't because you're too young. Would he ever fit in this puzzle called Texas?

"It's not a trick, Baba," pled Joseph. "You wanted me to spend less time playing the piano and start doing man things. Football is a man's game."

"I said I wanted you to do grown-up things, Joseph. Serious things. A game is not a serious thing."

"But Baba . . ."

"It's okay," said Baba.

Joseph stopped and searched Baba's face.

"You can play. But if your English grades drop, it's over. And you can't play on Shabbat."

"Thank you, Baba-jun!" Joseph hugged Baba and Maman. They gave each other those wry smiles as if they knew it would be trouble later.

Maybe Joseph could earn a black-and-gold Hawks football jersey. Maybe Vonda Baer would notice. Maybe she'd want to wear it. And maybe he could get a step closer to retrieving six dollars and two cents and his dignity from the two dirty birds.

12
DIRT HELMET

"They're cousins," said Mateo. "Larry and Brian Edmondson. They should be a year ahead of us in school, but one family moved when they were in elementary school. When they moved back a couple of years later, that cousin was put in class with the other one, who'd been held back a year."

That explained why Grimy and Possum's muscles stood out on their arms and shoulders and they had more than peach fuzz on their legs. Joseph skipped a year because he was so good at math. He was tall, but his smooth skin proved he was still a seventh grader by age. He had strong muscles built in boxing class, but not like the Edmondsons'. Larry and Brian strutted through the gym locker room like two roosters.

Joseph watched Mateo dip an engine part in a cleaning solution. The Ybarras owned eighty acres on the outskirts of town where oil pumps slowly dipped like giant, hungry, steel hummingbirds. Mr. Ybarra was a horse trainer by morning, and he ran several head of cattle that served to train the roping horses. In the afternoons, Mr. Ybarra repaired small engines. The local motorcycle shop employed him to repair motorcycles when their own mechanic couldn't keep up. In the summertime, Mr. Ybarra did landscaping for a few customers in the evenings. Joseph had rarely seen him when he wasn't working. He kept the twins and their older brothers busy, too.

"The cousins are always together. Always trouble," said Mateo, "but Larry, the older one, calls the shots. Brian, the younger one, is the one who starts the trouble. I think Larry just keeps Brian from getting himself in bigger trouble."

Joseph liked the aromas of tire rubber, plastic, paint, and oil. Mateo and Roberto had dirt bikes, but they had to help in the repair shop. Roberto spent his money on motorcycle gear. Mateo saved his money. He planned to go to the University of Texas like his older brothers. One of the older brothers had left his dirt bike when he went to college, and Joseph rode it. It was a good fit since Joseph had long legs.

Mateo was super smart. Almost everyone liked him, even the white kids. Mateo made you feel as if you were his best friend. Joseph suspected Mateo put up with him because he was friends with Roberto, but sometimes he asked Joseph for help with math homework. He didn't want the answers, though. He wanted to understand how to solve the problem. The world was a place Mateo wanted to understand and put in better order.

The Ybarra twins were easy to tell apart. Roberto had a slightly smaller frame. High energy, fun, and mischief swirled around him like a cloud. Mateo was taller and larger. Even though he was only thirteen, Mateo had Mr. Ybarra's adult dignity. Only Mateo could run laps in gym like a Marine drill sergeant. No sweat. Mateo was elected class president the last two years in a row. He made Joseph feel like there was an adult present. When he and Roberto proposed some sketchier types of fun, Mateo overruled them. Mateo was their gang's "okay or *oy veh*," a term Joseph had learned in synagogue. If Mateo approved, okay. If not, oy veh, no way!

"Do the Edmondsons live in town?" asked Joseph.

"Not too far from you. They moved last summer from the government housing apartments to one of those funny old houses that have two sides and two entrance doors. The cousins play football, so they get away with a lot of things in school that people like us wouldn't." Mateo set the engine part on a shelf to dry. "Their dads both go to the honky-tonk at the edge of the county on Friday and Saturday nights."

"How do you know that?" asked Joseph.

"They drive by in an old blue GMC truck that's really beat up," said Roberto. "It's broken down on the highway a couple of times. They walked here to get Papi to come fix it."

"Yeah, and they didn't pay him," said Mateo. "They said they'd bring the money by later, but they never did." He washed his hands at the shop sink. Mateo didn't like working on the engines. Mateo would always have his head stuck in a book if he could.

"Weirdest thing, though," said Roberto. "We were out riding one evening early in the summer. We saw them driving a different pickup, and they were coming back to town on the Dallas highway. It was a nice truck, brand new. They turned down a road we've never been on. Later that night, they passed our house going to town from the direction of the honky-tonk, but they were in their old pickup."

"The Edmondsons bother you at football practice?" Mateo asked Joseph.

Joseph said, "Brian calls me Pretty Boy in the locker room, and Larry calls me Skinny Boy or Hey Kid if he has to speak to me. On the field, they don't pay any attention to me. A couple of times in the locker room Brian told me that we weren't done yet, and I better watch my back because I messed up his bicycle wheel. Blows me kisses in the hallway. That's about it."

"I can do something about that," said Mateo. "Want to go ride?"

"Yeah," said Joseph. "Take me to where you saw the Edmondsons driving the truck. Maybe it has some good places to ride."

———

"It's posted," said Mateo over the idle of his bike. He pointed to the neat sign wrapped around the gatepole: *No Trespassing*. "We can't ride there."

"No, but look," said Joseph. "See all that green brush winding through the field? That means there's a creek. Maybe that's the property line, and we won't get in trouble if we ride down there. I want to find some mud."

"And there's some hills, too," said Roberto. "We can practice jumping our bikes. It's hard to practice whipping it without hills. We can ride on the pavement to the fence line. I'll bet if there's a creek, there's a gap in the fence."

"No," said Mateo. "It's clearly posted. There's a barn, and the gate to it is locked. That's a message to stay out. I'm going back. It will be time to feed the horses by the time we get back anyway." He turned and rode toward home.

Joseph knew that Mateo expected him and Roberto to follow. Instead, he and Roberto exchanged a look. Roberto put his bike in gear and rode slowly along the ditch line of the road. Sure enough, at the place where the snaking pattern of green brush met the road, there was a large pipe culvert. It allowed the water from the stream to flow under the county road. The gap between the barbed-wire fence and creek bed was more than enough room to ride under.

Roberto went first, and Joseph followed. The stream had cut a deep path through the fields. Once in the creek bed, they couldn't even see the level of the field above their heads. Scrub brush and short mesquite trees lined the sides, and wild grasses gave traction for their tires. It was probably full of ticks, though. Joseph hated ticks, but that was the price to pay for riding in the fields. Gloriously, though, there was mud. Mud could be washed off and muddy jeans thrown in the laundry hamper. Bugs burrowed into your tender bits and hung on.

About a hundred yards in, they came to the hills Roberto had seen. They were mounds of fresh earth on one side of the creek. "This doesn't look natural," said Joseph.

Roberto shook his head. There was nothing else like it around. "Someone dumped this dirt here with heavy equipment," he said.

"Wonder why they dumped it here? Where did it come from?" mused Joseph.

"Don't know, dude, but the playground's open," said Roberto, and he gunned his engine. For the next half hour, they tore over and through the mounds of earth above the creek bed, challenging one another to more dangerous jumps. They saved the highest mound for last. Roberto nodded to Joseph to try first. The grade of the hill was steeper than he'd thought, and Joseph's bike went sideways in the air. He kept his body in line with the front suspension and accelerated. The landing impact was hard, but Joseph kept his wrists straight and absorbed it with his legs and bent elbows. He brought the bike to a stop and turned to warn Roberto, but Roberto had already followed.

Roberto miscalculated the angle of approach. It kicked his bike off to the side. Roberto and his bike were suspended in the air forever before they crashed into separate rolls. The bike somersaulted over into the creek bed. Roberto didn't roll as far. Joseph abandoned his bike and ran to Roberto.

"You okay?" he asked.

Roberto tried to get up, but he only made it to his knees. "I think so."

"You sure?"

Roberto looked up and unsnapped his helmet. "Pretty sure."

Joseph scraped some dirt and grass from Roberto's helmet visor. "Looks like you dug a ditch with your head," said Joseph. He lifted under Roberto's arm, and Roberto stood unsteadily.

"I'm about a dumbass," Roberto said.

That gave Joseph a bit of relief. That was Roberto's usual pronouncement when someone did something stupid. It was usually, "*He's* about a dumbass," or "*You're* about a dumbass," but not "*I'm* about a dumbass."

"Let's go," said Joseph. "It's getting dark anyway. I'll help you with your chores before you take me back home."

Roberto nodded and walked toward the edge of the dirt mounds to look for his dirt bike below. Joseph pushed his to the edge, too. Roberto's bike lay about halfway down the bank. Together they slid down to it. It looked okay other than some dirt clods wedged in it, but it wouldn't start. Nothing. Roberto checked here and there to see if anything was damaged, but the descending darkness made it harder. After tinkering for several minutes, Roberto announced, "It's the plug wire. Nothing horrible, but I have to have a new one, or at least a working used one."

"What do we do?" asked Joseph.

"We'll have to leave it here. Hopefully, Papi won't notice it's missing. Maybe I can sneak back down here tonight after everyone's in bed. If I bring a flashlight, then I can change the plug wire and ride it back home. I'll cut the engine before I get home and push it into the workshop so Papi won't hear."

"It would take you all night to walk back here," objected Joseph. "Maybe Mateo would give you a ride."

"No, Mateo's leaving in the morning to go to Austin with the Junior National Honor Society. They're touring the capitol and meeting the governor and politicians."

Joseph stared at him, and Roberto's brown eyes glittered in the twilight. Was he hurting from the tumble? Frustrated? Maybe both.

"I know what to do," said Joseph.

Roberto didn't even answer.

"What time do your parents go to sleep?" asked Joseph.

"Around 10:30 p.m. 11:30 at the latest."

"Take Mateo's bike and pick me up at the railroad tracks at 1:00 a.m. We'll ride out here, you can fix your bike, and then we'll ride the bikes back to your place. You can bring me back to town, then go back home. It might take all night, but your parents won't know as long as no one wakes up and notices we're gone."

Roberto's eyes still glittered, but Joseph could sense a hopeful grin. A dangerous plan was better than no plan. "You're about a dumbass," said Roberto, but this time it was a compliment.

13
NIGHT CAP

They left Roberto's dirt bike hidden under some brush. Roberto rode with Joseph to Joseph's house to drop him off before Roberto rode the bike home. It was against traffic laws to ride a dirt bike on the roads, but that was the thing about Texas. There were laws, and there were *laws*. If there was no trouble, there was no trouble. The Ybarras made sure their dirt bikes weren't loud, and they didn't gun the engines in town, so no one ever complained. Boys will be boys. Hazel wasn't Dallas.

Maman fussed a little about how Joseph was so dirty and missed supper. Other than that, there was no problem. Maman had miscarried several babies before she and Baba had Joseph, so he got away with a lot of stuff that a normal kid would get punished for. There were so many things he couldn't do because of their religion that Joseph figured he was entitled to a reasonable amount of mischief.

While he showered, Maman reheated a bowl of *bamieh* with extra rice. Joseph needed to sleep a little before he sneaked out of the house, but he lay on the bed that night and thought through the plan. Walking through town in the daylight was one thing, but walking through town after midnight wasn't something he'd ever tried. That reminded him. He'd need a flashlight. He tried to slip into the kitchen to get the flashlight out of the drawer, but Maman heard him.

"Youssef, are you still hungry? Do you want me to heat up some more food?" she called from the hallway.

"It's okay, Maman," he called back. "Just getting a drink of water." He pulled open a cabinet door and took down a glass. After her bedroom door closed, Joseph turned on the water, using the sound of the water to cover the clatter of his plundering in the drawer for the flashlight. What if she came back into the hallway and saw him holding the flashlight? Joseph tucked it into the waistband of his shorts, but it tumbled onto the hardwood floor just as he turned into his bedroom.

"Youssef?" called Maman.

"I'm fine, Maman-jun. Just dropped something. Good night."

Thankfully, she didn't get up to check on him.

Although he didn't think he could possibly sleep, Joseph did doze off a few times. He'd jerk himself awake to check the clock. 11:13 p.m. 11:49 p.m. 12:31 a.m.

Oh, no! He should have started getting dressed at 12:15 a.m. It would take him a good thirty minutes to walk to the railroad tracks. Quickly, Joseph threw on the jeans and T-shirt he'd concealed under his bed and tied his sneakers in the dark. Fighting impatience to make up lost time, he slid the window up carefully, stopping to listen for any sound from Maman's room.

The drop to the ground was too far for him to close the window back, so he prayed she wouldn't check his room in the night. Joseph slid out the window feet first. He balanced on his belly to pull down the window sash as far as he could before he slithered down. Mosquitoes would probably swarm in the open window.

The neighborhood was bathed in the weird orange light of streetlamps. Joseph hurried down the sidewalk. Once he reached the feed store, he was out of range of regular lighting. The buildings were farther apart. It was spooky, reminding him of the scene in *To Kill a Mockingbird* when Jem, Scout, and Dill crept to Boo Radley's house. As if on cue, a dark, pulsing cloud flew out of a tall myrtle hedge right over his head.

Joseph ducked, clutching the flashlight defensively. Every curse word he knew rolled out unchecked. He squatted for several seconds on the road next to the hedge until his logical mind could convince his pounding heart that he'd only scared some roosting birds. His English teacher, Mrs. Thornton, would want to know the theme of the story, something Joseph never could figure out. This time it was easy. The theme was that birds really do sleep at night and you'd best be ready to be scared out of your wits if you wake them up.

If he hurried, he could outpace visions of chainsaw killers, cat burglars, and crazy men named Boo hiding trinkets in oak trees. Okay, forget walking. Joseph jogged the last quarter mile. Roberto was already at the railroad tracks, and Joseph climbed behind him nonchalantly, as if he hadn't been scared witless by some birds and wasn't sweating from his jog. "*¿Problema?*" asked Roberto.

"Nah."

After the long walk to the edge of town alone, the ride with Roberto to the property flew by. It was almost a full moon, so once his eyes adjusted, it was pretty easy to see. They met a few

oncoming cars, but Roberto pulled down into the roadside
ditch. They idled as still as statues until the headlights passed.
When they reached the big culvert, they puttered down into the
creek bed and under the barbed-wire fence. They followed the
edge of the creek all the way to the brush where they'd stashed
Roberto's dirt bike.

It took only ten minutes for Roberto to replace the damaged
plug wire while Joseph held the flashlight. Joseph urged, "See
if it will start."

Just then, they heard something. "Shhh . . . wait," said
Joseph. "*Cállate.*"

It was the sound of clanking metal, not a natural sound in
a field at night. Joseph shook away the image of a chainsaw and
listened. There was the sound of chains, but also the sound of a
truck idling. Supposedly ghosts rattled chains, but Joseph had
never heard of them driving trucks in dire need of a tune-up.

Joseph inched his way up the creek bank, and Roberto
followed. This time the metal crashed loudly, the sound of a
chain falling into a metal gate. Just above them, there should be
a cattle gate on the lane to the old barn in the field. Who would
be coming to a barn in the middle of the night?

Having already been bested by boos and birds of the night,
Joseph slowed his pace. Roberto crept ahead of him to peer over
the bank. When Joseph reached the top, Roberto crouched and
used a dirt hill to move closer. Joseph didn't want to get closer,
but he followed.

A truck sat at the cattle gate with its headlights off. A dark
figure pushed open the gate, and the truck pulled forward.
Whoever was holding the gate shut it behind the truck, but he
didn't padlock it.

"It's the Edmondson cousins' fathers," whispered Roberto. "I recognize the truck."

"What are they doing here in the middle of the night?" asked Joseph.

No answer.

The figure who'd shut the gate got in the passenger side, and the truck pulled up to the barn. Again, the passenger got out and opened the barn door. The truck slowly pulled in, and the passenger followed it inside, shutting the barn door behind him.

"Let's go," said Joseph. "We can push the bikes out to the road, and they won't hear us start them."

"I want to see what they're doing," said Roberto. "Let's sneak into the side shed. Maybe we can see through the boards."

"No," said Joseph.

"Why not?"

"There's ticks in that tall grass."

"We've snuck out of our houses in the middle of the night onto private property on a school night, but you're worried about *ticks*?"

At least Roberto didn't call him a dumbass.

"Come on. They'll never know we're here," urged Roberto.

"Alright," said Joseph, but it wasn't. Before Roberto could think he was scared, Joseph crawled into the grass first. It was wet with dew and top-heavy with late-summer seed. His jeans would be soaked within half a minute.

Roberto fell in behind him, and they crawled to the sagging shed attached to the main barn. It was full of ancient round bales of hay taller than Joseph. That gave him some comfort as he knelt in their musty shadows. Cobwebs everywhere. And bugs. Joseph could feel things crawling all over him.

14

COWBOY HAT

Voices came from inside the barn. Suddenly, a small generator started. Lights flashed on. Roberto and Joseph both found gaps in the boards and peered in. "That's the truck we saw them driving from Dallas that night," whispered Roberto.

Inside were more round bales of hay. In the loft were hundreds of smaller square bales connected by blankets of spider webs. And probably ticks. Chiggers were bad because they'd eat a circle around your ankles, but ticks traveled inside your clothes and went up to the penthouse suite.

Joseph's eyes followed the movement inside the barn. It was easy to tell the two men inside were brothers. Both had brown, straight hair, and both wore jeans, T-shirts, and greasy ballcaps. That would explain Larry's dirty lid.

An old gray plank door to a room stood open, what Joseph guessed was an old feed room. That was where the generator sound was coming from. Both men disappeared inside, then reemerged a few minutes later. This time they both wore new jeans, Western-style dress shirts with bolo ties, expensive boots, and cowboy hats. What the heck?

The new Ford pickup was a red dually made for pulling livestock trailers. One of the men jumped into the bed of the truck and unlocked the toolbox behind the cab. He removed the top trays, lots of tools, and then some flat metal pieces. Afterward, he caught several white cube-like bundles thrown to him from the other man. He packed them deeply into the toolbox, eventually replacing the flat metal pieces over the top of them. Finally, he arranged all the tools back in the box and reset the trays. Joseph worried about the time. Should they go, or wait to see if the Edmondsons would leave?

His question was answered when the man in the bed of the truck locked the toolbox and jumped down. He closed the tailgate while the other man cut the generator and closed the storeroom door. They exited the way they came in, this time driving the shiny, red pickup back out to the highway. Only when the truck was on the paved road did its headlights come on.

"What was that?" asked Joseph, brushing away and scratching at what he was sure were hundreds of insects crawling up his clothes.

"Drugs," said Roberto.

"How do you know that?" asked Joseph.

"You don't watch *Hawaii Five-O*?" asked Roberto. "Or *Starsky & Hutch*?"

"No," admitted Joseph. They didn't have a television. Baba let him go to the movies occasionally. He'd seen *Star Wars*. Three times. Baba only knew about one time.

"Come on," said Roberto.

Roberto always wanted to push the edge, but tonight, Joseph wished that Mateo were here. They needed a grown-up.

Joseph trailed Roberto to a single entrance door from the shed into the barn, swatting at bugs and hating the feel of the heavy, clammy-wet jeans on his legs. If he could just get out of this, he'd go on no more night rides with Roberto.

"Use your flashlight," suggested Roberto. Joseph pulled the flashlight from his back pocket. "Shine it on the storage room door." Joseph aimed the light, and together they pulled open the wooden plank door. Inside was the generator. Two garment bags hung from nails, and two hat carriers sat on a bench along with the old clothes and shoes. Joseph worked the flashlight around until Roberto caught his wrist and aimed the light. "There."

It was an old wooden feed bin. Roberto lifted the lid and looked inside. There was nothing but a big empty box, but it wasn't as dusty as it should have been. Roberto got on his knees and pulled at the bottom until it popped out of place. He tugged up, and Joseph aimed the flashlight down into inky darkness.

"I'm going," said Roberto.

"No, let's get out of here," said Joseph. "We know there's drugs down there. That's enough."

"I want to see," said Roberto, and he threw a leg over into the feed trough. Once he'd found a foothold on the top rung, he steadied himself with one hand and beckoned for the flashlight with the other. Joseph handed it to him.

Roberto was down there for about five minutes, but in the darkness, it felt endless to Joseph. When Roberto climbed back up, he handed Joseph the flashlight. "It's drugs in a big room. They've dug a whole basement down there. They're still digging in places with shovels, I guess making more room. There's piles of those packages. One of them was open on a table. Those guys are taking drugs somewhere, probably Dallas. There's only two choices at the crossroads: town or the highway to the interstate."

"We need to get out of here," said Joseph.

"Yeah," said Roberto. "Let's get it all back like it was and get outta here."

And they did. Afterward, they pushed their dirt bikes down the streambed out to the ditch by the county road. Roberto's started on the third try. They raced back toward the Ybarra ranch, stopping only once to play statue with a passing car. Joseph was comforted by the thought that the Edmondsons had gone in the opposite direction. Even though they had no way of knowing if they'd been watched, it still *felt* as though they should know. You can't unknow what you know even if other people don't know you know.

With a hundred yards left to go to the Ybarra house, they cut their engines. Roberto pushed his bike to the workshop. He returned about ten minutes later, and Joseph scooted back to let Roberto on ahead of him. Ten minutes alone with the ticks was too long.

"My papá gets up at 5:00 a.m. to feed the horses," said Roberto. "I have to hurry, or he'll see me or hear me come back."

"Go as fast as you want," said Joseph.

Roberto opened up the dirt bike, expertly avoiding mailboxes and trash cans on the side of the highway. He dropped Joseph off a block from his house. Joseph eased home, no longer afraid of birds, boos, or chainsaws in the dark.

An angry, worried mother would be much worse, especially when she told his angry, angry father on Friday. When he reached his bedroom window, Joseph realized he had a problem.

He'd closed the window sash partway on his way out, and now he had the added weight of wet jeans. Oy veh. The gas meter was just a little too far away to use for a boost. *So jump*, Joseph told himself. *Just watch your . . .*

Owwwww. Joseph stood completely still, hoping Maman hadn't heard him hit his head on the window. Hard. He wasn't about to try that twice. There was no way he was getting back in the window with the sash that far down. He needed something to push it up. There was plenty of stuff in the garage, but he couldn't remember if the side door to the garage was unlocked. The house was silent, but a car passed in the predawn, and Joseph pressed himself into the shadows. A neighbor calling the police about a prowler would be a thousand times worse than Maman telling Baba he'd sneaked out of the house at night.

After he made sure there were no more cars, Joseph retrieved an old broom from the back porch and used it to push up the sash. He propped the broom against the sill before he jumped. One good jump, and he flopped over the sill on his belly. He tilted his head down until his hands touched the floor, then he slowly worked himself in until he could throw a leg over and stand up. After stopping to listen again for Maman, he pulled the broom inside and eased the window back down. It was almost shut when he heard Maman's footsteps in the hallway.

Joseph was too tall to scamper anywhere, but that's what he did, wet jeans and all, straight to his bed. He slid the broom underneath it and rolled in, pulled the covers high, and turned away from the door. The door clicked open softly. Joseph felt Maman's eyes searching the dark room. A soft sigh, then muted footfalls to the window. He heard it slide shut, and footsteps approached the side of his bed. Joseph pretended to sleep.

Maman's fingers tenderly brushed his hair. Then she was gone, pulling the door shut quietly behind her.

Only then could he breathe. The fading footsteps moved toward the kitchen, and Joseph could see the faint light come on under his bedroom door. What would he do with these wet clothes? Joseph slipped out of bed, stripped, and shoved the bundle of clothes under his bed as far as it would go. He'd figure out a way to dry them later and put them in the laundry. And that was it. Other than a sore head and the itch of mostly imaginary chiggers and ticks, he was home free.

15
SAFETY HELMET

"Maman, why do the letters from Iran come through California?" asked Joseph.

"They have to be reposted," said Maman in that tone that meant she didn't want to talk about it. She placed the new letter in the box with all the older ones. Every couple of months, she collected the Iranian letters in a big envelope and sent them to Joseph's uncles in Israel. She placed the bar mitzvah RSVPs in a separate pile.

"Why?"

There was a long silence. Maman answered things in her own time. She considered everything, collecting information endlessly before making a decision. Joseph didn't think his question should require that much mental research. Why wouldn't relatives from Iran send the letters directly to Texas?

"When we left Iran, it was to escape the Shah's secret police. We lost everything. Sometimes . . ." her voice faded. Maybe she was still collecting the information for her answer. It was maddening sometimes. Like whether she'd sign the release form so Joseph could play football. She'd made Baba read every single form, disclosure, and information sheet in the envelope and translate it into Farsi.

"Sometimes what?" Joseph prompted.

"We worry that . . ."

Another fade.

"It's safer." This time Maman said it confidently, a sentence with a period at the end.

"How is it safer?"

"Youssef-jun, you're too young to understand. It's safer for us if the letters go to relatives in California. They can read the news, and then they send them in new envelopes here. I send them to my brothers. That way all the news from home in Iran is shared."

Okay, Joseph knew that last part was made up. "Safer" and "secret police" were completely different answers than "shared news." Maman probably wouldn't say more now that she'd constructed a believable answer that he didn't believe. That was okay. Now Joseph knew where to start chipping away. He'd have to report the new clues to Shahla. Maybe he could pry some information out of one of his Israeli uncles at his bar mitzvah.

Something about those letters was safe for relatives in California, but not for them. Secret police. Safer. Losing everything. Joseph would find out. In the meantime, he had been studying hard for his bar mitzvah. This year, Joseph's birthday fell on Rosh Hashanah, the Jewish New Year. His bar mitzvah would take place in the synagogue on the following Friday afternoon and Shabbat, a day before Yom Kippur.

The bar mitzvah had to sing a section from the Torah and

a passage from the Prophets, called the *haftara*. The Hebrew words to the Torah and Prophets had to be sung according to cantillation marks, like musical notes. Joseph sneaked to LaLa's house several times to play the notes on her piano. It was easier to learn the notes and sing them that way. The Torah passage that stumped Joseph was:

"And die on the mountain that you are climbing, and be gathered to your people . . ."

The notes were odd, defying an easy cadence. The Hebrew phrase *oo-muht* was "And die," and it was as slippery as the word itself, cloaked in darkness. It was not often that Joseph couldn't pull notes easily from his memory, but he'd never had this kind of pressure. LaLa's piano recitals were on Saturday afternoons. Shabbat. He'd never participated in a recital with all the pressure of students and parents watching his performance.

Rabbi Rothstein was okay with Mr. Ybarra bringing the twins and LaLa to attend the Friday celebration. Mateo wanted to know if there was a book he could read to prepare. Roberto wanted to know if there would be food and a live band. If not, he volunteered to connect Baba with a really good mariachi band that had an accordion player. Joseph didn't pass Roberto's offer along. Baba had hired a three-piece Persian band from a big Persian community near Los Angeles. They'd arrive with all their instruments on the Amtrak train's Texas Eagle from LA to Dallas.

It would be Joseph's first year to fast completely on Yom Kippur. With a bellyful of bar mitzvah and Shabbat food, maybe it wouldn't be so bad. If he bungled the singing of the Torah and haftara, he'd also have a bellyful of embarrassment to digest for much longer. He couldn't shame Baba like that in front of their family and the whole synagogue. How could Joseph go through the rest of his life knowing he'd fouled up his very first responsibility as a Jewish man? No pressure there.

The part of his bar mitzvah he most looked forward to was seeing Shahla. Well, that and the presents. Joseph wasn't sure why he had so much affection for a girl cousin. Maybe it was because Maman was so fond of her. Shahla was flying in from California, and they wouldn't have to rely on their usual game of guessing what the other was thinking.

Their other game was to record everything they'd ever done together that was a first, like eating Persian *tahdig* with chopsticks. Surely no one had ever thought of that before. Maybe there would be some firsts at his bar mitzvah. Having a Persian bar mitzvah was probably a first for the Dallas synagogue.

After Baba and Maman, Shahla was the one Joseph wanted to see him execute his bar mitzvah perfectly. He wanted to impress her with something more than pranks, to show her he wasn't a kid anymore and he didn't just hover around Baba during prayers.

They picked up Shahla Thursday afternoon at the airport. While Baba put her little suitcase in the trunk, Maman and Joseph embraced her and kissed her cheeks. Like Joseph's, hers were rosy and her skin tone was richly caramel. They all three started speaking in Farsi at once. As usual, it was Shahla who fell silent first. "You can talk in the car," Baba said reprovingly, but he also stopped and kissed Shahla's cheeks with affection.

Shahla handed Joseph a box wrapped in shiny blue paper with a big white bow. She'd carried it so it wouldn't be crushed in her baggage. "You already know what's in it," she said. "I put Mateo and Roberto's in there, too, but you can pick which one you want." Joseph hugged her and kissed her cheeks again.

They drove to the reception hall at the synagogue where Joseph's bar mitzvah party would be held. Baba had flown in the caterer from Beverly Hills the day before. Maman assembled all the ingredients, and the caterer cooked Persian dishes in the synagogue kitchen all day. Rabbi Rothstein argued until Baba gave him a copy of the caterer's kosher certification. That was Baba. Quiet, but stubborn. And prepared. There was no way he'd serve European Jewish dishes like gefilte fish to the family. Maman shuddered at the mere mention of it.

That night, Joseph and Shahla worked together hanging glittery blue paper stars, Torah scrolls, and crowns from the ceiling. Vonda's eyes glittered blue in Joseph's thoughts, and he wished that she could come to his bar mitzvah.

"Did you have to miss school to come?" Joseph asked Shahla.

"Yeah," said Shahla, who retwisted a paper clip to make it flat before she hung a star. "It's okay, though. I can catch up pretty easy."

Joseph wondered if that were true. He'd been skipped a grade, but she'd nearly been kept back in kindergarten. She'd hardly heard any English before she started school, but Baba had made sure he spoke to Joseph in English as much as possible. Shahla was smart, though. Once she caught on to how to do something, she eventually ended up doing it better than him.

"Where's the rest of the family staying?" asked Shahla.

"A hotel within walking distance of the synagogue," said Joseph. "Although some of them drive on Shabbat. Maman says that some of them only go to synagogue on holidays."

"Oh," said Shahla.

Joseph asked, "Say, do you ever get to read the letters from our relatives in Iran?"

The silence told him she didn't. She finally asked, "What letters?"

"I don't know," said Joseph. "Sometimes we get letters."

"Oh."

A long silence followed. Joseph could have kicked himself for bringing it up. She was out of the loop. He always knew more about their Los Angeles relatives than she did even though she lived there.

"Was your Torah portion hard to learn?" she asked. She changed the subject to save him the embarrassment, but Joseph still wished he hadn't brought it up.

"It was hard to learn the cantillation. I'm afraid I'll forget the first note, and then I'll go blank. I had to memorize the Preamble to the Constitution for civics class last year. Half the time when I look at the first word, I think 'We the People of the United States . . .'"

Shahla looked down from her position on the ladder. "You never forget music," she said. "I'm going to hit you with candy after you finish reading. Hard."

If she tried, she'd do it. Shahla's arm was as accurate as Joseph's. He'd taught her to play basketball. He knew the consequences of missing a low pass from her. "Maybe I'd better put my football helmet on," Joseph joked.

"You can't wear it forever," said Shahla. "I'll get you eventually."

Joseph couldn't disagree with that. She'd fired the opening shot, so he really was off his game. He couldn't let his nerves get the best of him. "I ate so much apples and honey last week for Rosh Hashanah that I'm still pissing apple juice," said Joseph.

"Youssef!" said Shahla. "What if your maman heard you?"

"You seriously think she'd know what it meant in English?" asked Joseph.

"She may not know exactly, but if it comes out of *your* mouth, she could guess," said Shahla.

Joseph grinned in triumph. Their time together was back to its usual start.

"Switch with me," she said. "My arms are tired." She climbed down from the ladder and Joseph climbed up.

"It's shaky," he said. "Hold it tighter."

"I'm right here," she said. "I won't let you fall."

16
THE CROWN

The next morning was organized chaos. The reception hall should have been under a tornado weather alert. Sound the sirens. Baba picked up the band and helped them set up in the reception hall. It was the biggest headache of the day. He had to drive to a local music store to buy more connectors and cables that didn't make it from California to Dallas on the train. In between, Baba met with Rabbi Rothstein, who came in to make sure the synagogue sanctuary was in order. He hovered around the kosher caterer in the kitchen under the pretense of being helpful. Joseph was sure he was just being nosy.

Maman organized the meals, fussing over which meal should be heavier since everyone was preparing to fast for Yom Kippur. Joseph was sure it was better to load his belly with as much as it could hold, but Maman insisted he stay away from heavy foods. Shahla said it wasn't bad if you stayed busy. She'd been fasting on Yom Kippur for a few years, but she didn't eat that much to begin with. Baba assured Joseph that there were so many prayers on Yom Kippur that it would keep him occupied and his mind off his growling stomach. Joseph knew that wasn't true. Baba's stomach always growled on Yom Kippur, and you couldn't be within ten feet of him without your mind being on it.

At lunchtime, Baba, Maman, Shahla, and Joseph went back to the apartment to shower and dress. There was nervous energy in the small apartment, and it swirled around Joseph. When Maman offered him a tuna sandwich with the little pickles he liked, he only nibbled half of it. For the first time, Shahla finished his lunch instead of him finishing hers. "That's a first for us," she said.

Joseph nodded.

"Nervous?" she asked casually, as if dread weren't about to squeeze him into a little ball, which would be fine, so he could roll out of sight.

"Nah," said Joseph.

"Liar," said Shahla.

"Hey . . ." Joseph started to protest, but she grinned. She was trying to get his mind off the job ahead, which was to not embarrass his whole family.

Joseph shook his head. "I'm trying to practice the Torah portion in my head, but all I keep getting is 'We the People of the United States . . .' If I can't get the words right, then I'll never remember the starting note. And if I get the note, what if my voice cracks? When Morty Silver did it last month, he butchered it."

"Yeah, but everyone cheered anyway, right? Come on," said Shahla. "We'll sing it together." She started in the key he'd been practicing, "*Vaidaber Adonai el Moshe . . .*" Joseph joined in, and they sang through the whole reading.

Shahla always knew how to take the edge off. Maybe it would be okay.

The synagogue was nearly full. Rabbi Rothstein gave a little welcome speech for the special occasion. He then called up Joseph and Baba. When Baba handed Joseph his new tallit, a prayer shawl, it was with the pride of a thousand shining jewels in his hand. It was folded, tightly square from its packaging. Joseph took it, shook it open, and whispered the blessing. He made the accordion folds like he'd practiced with Baba's. Smile when you're angry. Smile when you're terrified. It's all under control. The fabric felt heavy on his shoulders. Maybe it was because Baba and the rabbi always added the burden of three thousand years of Jewish tradition in their bar mitzvah lessons.

Next came the black leather straps of the tefillin, one for his arm and one for his head. Rabbi Rothstein put on Joseph's hand-tefillin, leaving the end loose. Baba helped him put on his head-tefillin while Joseph made the blessing. The rabbi finished the loop of the hand-tefillin, and he squeezed Joseph's hand gently when he felt it shaking. Joseph felt both ridiculous and proud.

Rabbi Rothstein took out the Torah scroll and passed it to Baba, then Baba to Joseph. And then came the silver crown. Carefully, reverently, Rabbi Rothstein fit the silver crown over the top of the scroll. Joseph carried the scroll around the men's section so they could touch the fringes of their tallits to it. This was something Joseph really couldn't mess up unless he threw the scroll down and ran in the other direction. He smiled as if he knew exactly what he was doing. Roberto would be impressed; that is, if he hadn't seen Joseph's hands shaking.

When he passed by the women's section, Joseph paused a little longer near Maman and Shahla so they could touch their prayer books to the scroll. Maman cried and smiled at the same time. Shahla rubbed Maman's back, sharing her joy. With Maman's help, Shahla's long, curly black hair had been wound up into a very grown-up chignon that left her slender neck exposed. Joseph would have to keep an eye on Roberto. A pretty girl a shade darker than Shahla was standing next to her and Maman. Joseph wondered who she was. There weren't many brown Jews in Texas.

During this royal march around the synagogue, Joseph noticed two of his Israeli uncles and a cousin. They had stationed themselves at the exit doors of the sanctuary. That was weird, but Joseph couldn't afford to be distracted by it. They'd served in the Israeli army, and they were gung ho on security way more than Americans.

Joseph carried the scroll back to the *bimah*, a high, wooden bench where the rabbi would unroll the scroll so he could read it. Joseph wondered if little Morty Silver had to stand on his tiptoes during his reading. That might account for why he sounded like a drunken parrot.

This was the part that could go so badly wrong. So many steps, words, notes . . . *We the People of the United States* . . . The rabbi removed the silver crown, removed the embroidered velvet Torah cover, and unrolled the scroll on the bimah. He slid a silver pointer down the Hebrew letters flowing like an inky black river across the pale parchment. When Rabbi Rothstein found the place, he nodded to Joseph and handed him the pointer so he could keep his place as he read. Again, Joseph's hand was shaking. Baba moved close beside him, his warmth and clove scent penetrating the fabric of both their tallits.

Steps. Steps. Everything had to go in steps. *We the People of the United States, in Order to form a more perfect Union . . .* Joseph set down the pointer, closed the scroll, and tried to remember the blessing. Ten tunes and blessings swam through his mind. Miraculously, the right tune with the right words tread water long enough for him to snatch them out and deliver them safely. After he chanted the blessing, Baba smiled. His voice hadn't cracked. One tiny terror down. Several big ones to go. Joseph reopened the scroll and found his place with the silver pointer. This was it.

17
RAIN HAT

Joseph's hand shook so badly that he covered the first word with the pointer. He closed his eyes and put himself back into the apartment so he could hear Shahla's voice. Would those notes come out of his mouth, or some wrecked Polly-want-a-cracker?

Vaidaber Adonai el Moshe veh-etzem ha-yom hazeh le-emor.

Yes! He'd hit it clearly. The first verse was out. Then the second one, a difficult one because of the brokenness that preceded the sadness of the next one. He did it. Now the hard one, "And die on this mountain you are climbing . . ." The notes went from the difficult low ones and climbed to the high ones, challenging his voice. His hand shook so much that the silver pointer moved in a zigzag under the words instead of a line.

Joseph sang. He grabbed each word, catching the tide of the words, rolling through them more rapidly until he gained the speed of a real song, like Baba. The wind of confidence drove him more surely through the story about the end of Moses's life.

About midway through, Joseph gained so much confidence

that he sang as if he were in LaLa's parlor, strong and soulful. It was actually fun. Well, almost. More like a roller coaster ride with all the fear of plunging into the unexpected drop of a mental lapse. He could feel the smiles directed at him, his baba's pride, and Joseph's dread turned to a kind of giddiness. When he finished, Joseph closed the scroll for the blessing. Candy flew at him from everywhere. The Persian women ululated, and everyone cheered.

Afterward, all the men sang "Siman Tov Mazal Tov" and enveloped him in a joyous circle dance. Rabbi Rothstein alternately shook his head and nodded, his funny way of showing approval. Baba pressed his hands onto Joseph's head and blessed him before he helped him remove the tefillin and place them in their soft velvet storage bag.

Rabbi Rothstein addressed the synagogue: "It's customary for the bar mitzvah to deliver a speech. His speech is a thought from his Torah portion, which the young man will explain applies in some way to his own life. So now, I present to you Youssef Nissan, son of Kamran and Miriam Nissan, who will encourage us with a few words from his reading."

Joseph took a folded piece of notebook paper from his inside suit pocket. Now that the worst was over, he wasn't afraid. He began, "Welcome to my family from Israel and California and my friends from synagogue and from Hazel. First, I'd like to thank my baba and Rabbi Rothstein for their help preparing me for my bar mitzvah. That had to be more painful for them than it was for me."

They both nodded in agreement, and Joseph heard some snickers from the audience.

"And thanks to Maman for all her hard work preparing the

food, the invitations, and decorations . . . and for listening to me sing my portion like a million times."

The ladies in the women's section nodded at Maman knowingly, and she smiled.

"I'll try to keep this short because I know that you're all looking forward to the upcoming fast for Yom Kippur, and you need lots of time to think about how hungry you'll be."

Everyone laughed.

Joseph continued. "My Torah portion is *Ha'azinu*, or 'Give ear.' That sounds like Shakespeare to me when you say it in English, but then again, when you read it in Hebrew, it sounds like Yoda talking. My English teacher would have a fit."

Just about everybody laughed at that except the rabbi and Baba.

"But I think the big thing is that we need to listen to words. They're important. Moses taught the Israelites a song before he died. When I thought of it that way, it made sense to 'Give ear.' People are learning a song. After all, some musicians 'play by ear.'" Joseph glanced at Baba, but he didn't frown, and Joseph went on.

"When I don't listen to Baba, he gives me a *gooshmali*, a pull on my ear. People who don't like to plan or read music sometimes 'play it by ear.' I'm betting some of my Israeli relatives don't understand exactly what I mean by some of those words."

The Israelis murmured agreement.

"Words can make things easy to understand, or they can make them hard. If you've ever tried translating for someone, you know that."

Many more heads nodded in agreement.

"Moses solved the problem of how to help the Israelites understand his final words by teaching them a song."

Baba shifted and frowned a little. Oy veh.

Joseph returned his eyes to his notes. "So what do we need to do to hear Moses's song, or any song? According to Moses, the answer is rain. He said, 'Give ear, O heavens, and I will speak; and hear, O earth, the words of my mouth. My doctrine shall drop as the rain, my speech shall distill as the dew, as the small rain upon the tender herb, and as the showers upon the grass.'

"So, the way to hear good words is to soak them up. Rain doesn't do any good unless the grass soaks it up and turns green. That means we need to say good words and soak up good words. Let words change us and make us better people. When Moses died, it says in Hebrew that his moisture had not decreased. I think that means that he was still able to hear from God and from other people. He wasn't a stubborn guy, you know? He listened to people. He said good words and he received good words."

Baba relaxed. This wasn't turning into a public appeal for piano privileges. Joseph continued, "Recently I've run into some people who speak a lot of bad words. They call people names and try to embarrass them. Because I was wearing a kippah, I was called words that Baba won't let me say in the synagogue . . . well, he won't let me say them at home, either. And really, I don't think those words should be said anywhere to anyone. Those words made me angry, and I got into a fight."

Baba shifted and frowned again. Oops.

"But Baba gave me some good advice. He said that there are always people who will hate Jews. I guess they'll hate anyone who is different. But Baba said there are always a few good people, and I should find them. I think these are the people who use good words to encourage others, not to humiliate them. These people are here today for me, and I hope that I can always be there for them. Thank you all for coming and reminding me that good words and good people go together. I hope to find many more as I go through life. Thank you."

Joseph knew the candy was coming, so he pulled his new tallit over his head protectively as he ducked Shahla's butterscotch missiles and the gentler showers of candy that accompanied the shouts of "Mazal Tov." He grinned and whispered to himself, ". . . do ordain and establish this Constitution for the United States of America."

18

HAT BAND

The reception was on the scale between upbeat and rowdy. A cousin informed Joseph that the local synagogue the family attended in Tehrangeles was fed up with the Persian immigrants. There was a proposal afoot to build them their own synagogue. Persians celebrated noisily, were prone to chatting during the service, and arrived late as a matter of course. It didn't go over well with American Jews.

Rabbi Rothstein and the older men from the synagogue looked a little frazzled by the Iranian invasion and Farsi fun. For the most part, everyone had a good time, the Persians more so than the others. Mr. Ybarra was there with the twins. He was dressed so nicely in a Western suit, expensive ostrich boots, and a bolo tie, that he was nearly unrecognizable.

Thanks to the new electric cables, the Persian band was loud. The men danced in circles with the other men, leaping, twirling, and swaying. A few showed off by doing handstands. Some of the teenagers took turns jumping into the middle of the circle to do the worm or break dance. Joseph was sure he'd end up in a double knot if he tried either. He stuck with the shoulder-to-shoulder rhythm of the circle.

The band shifted to Middle Eastern modals and a heavy drumbeat. Mateo was a good sport, but Roberto really got into it. With a little coaching, Roberto did pretty good with the Persian dances. They required spreading and loosening one's arms and hands and letting them undulate to the music. Morty Silver also danced like a drunken parrot, so beside him, Roberto looked like a professional.

Eventually, the men formed two lines facing one another across their side of the floor, and the two men at the end grabbed Joseph. With locked hands, they tossed him forward on his belly. It was a good thing he hadn't eaten yet. That would make anyone lose his baba ganoush. Baba waited for him at the end, and the group collapsed around them. Joseph looked around for Rabbi Rothstein, but he didn't see him. Maybe he'd taken a break from the Middle Eastern madness in his reception hall, or maybe he'd gone to his office to use his private bathroom. Must be nice.

Mateo returned to a table with Mr. Ybarra and LaLa, and they sat enjoying the hilarity. Mateo was probably taking mental notes for a social studies report on other cultures. LaLa was likely analyzing the band's Middle Eastern style and testing it against her music textbook's theory on Phrygian modals. No typewriter obituary music today. Surely her fall and spring recitals would be more interesting with some Middle Eastern music. Recitals Baba would never let Joseph be in.

When Joseph noticed his Israeli uncle Eli sampling the sweets, he joined him at the buffet. Time for the plan. Joseph grabbed a dessert plate and pretended to give the piles of honey-soaked pastries a careful look. "You sing as well as your father," said Uncle Eli. "I'll make sure you are called up for an *aliyah* at our synagogue when you come visit next summer." The unwanted honor was sealed with a hearty, one-armed hug, and Joseph thought he felt something hard on his uncle's hip. A gun? Seriously?

Shake it off, Joseph thought to himself. *Work the plan. Ask him.* "Uncle Eli, do you think we'll ever go back to Iran? I'd like to visit the synagogue in Tehran." There. Could there be any cleverer way to get Uncle Eli to say why they really left Iran?

What followed was a ten-minute Iranian history and politics lesson that made no sense at all. Uncle Eli gestured wildly, spilling baked sweets everywhere. He put down the plate when one hand wasn't enough to describe how Great Britain, France, Germany, and Russia had conspired to plunder a sovereign nation, and how greedy people and religious fanatics caused everything wrong in the world, and how it was impossible for a man to simply work a job and take care of his family in peace . . .

Uncle Eli was a human vacuum, and when anyone came close enough, Uncle Eli sucked them into the conversation. The little knot of men grew around the dessert table until it was swallowed. Joseph edged away. If there was an answer in Uncle Eli's rant, it was buried in the melee. The men practically shouted at one another and waved their arms. To an outsider, a fight was about to break out. To a Persian, it was a nice chat. To Joseph, it was a dead end.

Joseph put down the plate and went back to the dance floor until he grew hot and tired. He took a break and joined Shahla at the punch bowl when he noticed Roberto talking to her way too long. "Your papá is looking for you," Joseph said to Roberto.

Roberto grinned smugly. "No he isn't," he said, but he got the hint and wandered off.

Shahla rolled her eyes. "Bossy, aren't you?"

"Yeah," said Joseph. "You should be used to it by now."

"Cool it," she said, and handed him a cup of punch. "I can take care of myself. I'll talk to who I want to talk to."

"Not when I'm around," said Joseph.

Shahla threw a salted almond at him.

"Don't you think Maman's brothers from Israel are going a little too hard-core on this security thing?" asked Joseph. "I swear they are carrying pistols under those 1974 jackets. It's nearly 1980 for heaven's sake."

"They are," said Shahla matter-of-factly.

"How do you know?" asked Joseph.

"It's just security, Youssef. You're Jewish. You're in a synagogue. There's cars in the parking lot. Lots of people don't like Jews. You don't need to be an algebra whiz to figure that out. You can never have too much security," said Shahla.

"Yeah, but . . ."

Shahla cut him a look, and he remembered.

"Sorry," he said. "But where did they get pistols?"

Shahla shrugged in that way that said even if she knew, she wouldn't tell him. Why was she so far out of the loop on some things, but so informed on others? When it came to being cautious, she was off the charts like the Israelis. Maybe it was because of how her parents died. Even if she didn't know about the letters from Iran, maybe Shahla had picked up something they could piece together. Before he could ask her, Shahla went back to the women's side of the dance floor.

19
HIGH HAT

His bar mitzvah was the most Shabbastic day Joseph could remember. The pretty girl that Joseph saw sitting with Shahla in the women's section walked around with her. Joseph saw Maman's Israeli brothers talking to the girl's parents. It looked like more of an interrogation, but Israelis were kind of in your face like that. They wanted to know who you were and who you knew that they knew. Well, maybe that was more of a Jewish thing.

After an exhausting number of *yai-yai-yais*, Joseph took a break to eat something. He could eat light tomorrow to prepare for the fast. For now, he may as well load up on the abundance of Persian delicacies. After a cautious look around to make sure Uncle Eli wasn't near the buffet, Joseph filled his plate and took a seat across from Shahla and the new girl. "Hey," said Shahla in Farsi. "I found more Iranians, and I invited them. They're glad to hear people speaking Farsi." Shahla nodded to the girl, "Fereshteh, this is my cousin Youssef. He's the bar mitzvah boy . . . excuse me . . . man. Youssef, this is Fereshteh."

"Hello," said Joseph. The girl had glossy black hair and eyes of copper like a lioness. Her nose was fine, not the norm for Persians, who tended to have big noses. Maman's nose was a little big, but not bad. Baba's wasn't really big at all. Joseph checked his routinely to make sure his wasn't getting too big.

"Hello," said Fereshteh.

Shahla said, "Their family got out of Iran because things are getting so bad there. They ended up in Birmingham, Alabama, but then her father found a job in San Francisco, which is where they're headed now. They stopped off here in Dallas for Shabbat and ran right into a Persian party. What are the odds of that?"

"Pretty slim," said Joseph, who ran a few numbers in his head. No, you couldn't calculate it without knowing how many Persian Jews lived in Alabama or whether this unfortunate family was the only one. It would be totally nerdy to say so though, and he was no longer a nerd. He was a jock. A Jewish man. He hadn't missed a note or mispronounced one word in his Torah and haftara readings.

They chatted while they ate. When Shahla got up to go use the restroom, Joseph realized that Fereshteh's lioness eyes were more like a cornered cat's. She was FOB, a not-so-nice way that Los Angeles Persians referred to new immigrants. Fresh Off the Boat. Scared. Confused. Disoriented. Waiting for a fresh, steaming disaster of misunderstanding. Shahla was Fereshteh's tiny island of security in a room full of strangers. Without Shahla, she was alone again, and she looked around for her parents.

"So you're moving to San Francisco?" asked Joseph. "Are there Iranians there?"

Fereshteh's FOB look deepened. "I don't know. Baba says if there are Jews there, that's enough to help us get established in a community, but until today, we've not met many Jews in America like us."

Joseph nodded. He felt that burn in Hazel, but at least there were summer visits to Israel and occasional family events in LA. And there was Shahla to talk to every week and see at holidays. "How's your English?" asked Joseph.

Another shade of worry crossed the copper eyes. Wrong thing to ask.

"I'm learning, and Baba speaks a little. Maman . . . very little."

"My baba speaks really good English," said Joseph. "Maman understands a lot, but it's hard to get her to speak it. She should get out more, but it's hard to make friends in the town where we live."

"It looks like you have plenty of friends," said Fereshteh.

"That's the family from Los Angeles and some from Israel," said Joseph. "They congregate for this kind of thing." Joseph was getting tired of entertaining a sad girl, a girl facing hard times. Her life would get harder before it got easier. She needed something that she was good at to help her fit in, like math or football. Not much chance of that when you're FOB.

"So is school in America hard?" asked Fereshteh.

"Nah," said Joseph. "I mean, you have to figure out where you fit in and everything, and you'll have to take English as a second language, and it's hard to keep kosher in school . . ." Well, he wasn't encouraging her much.

"Maybe we could write back and forth, and you could coach me," said Fereshteh with all the hopeful sincerity of an abandoned puppy chasing every passing car up and down the highway.

"Are you kidding me?" said Joseph.

It came out wrong. All wrong. Her pretty face went from

sad and hopeful to complete embarrassment. She blushed and looked down.

"I'm sorry," said Joseph. "I mean . . . I have a girlfriend . . . and that's a long way to . . ."

Abruptly, she stood and spun away, disappearing into the crowd.

Joseph knew he'd done something deeply wrong. He pushed away the feeling and got up to dance so he didn't feel so mean. He danced only one dance before Shahla came up behind him and pulled him out of the men's circle by the ear. She didn't let up, either, and walked him out to the hallway. People grinned as Shahla pulled him along like a child leading a giraffe. Baba looked concerned, but he didn't give chase. Baba knew that if Shahla was mad at him, there was a pretty good reason. Maman was inspecting the food table inventory and mentally calculating the amount of food in reserve down to the gram, so she wasn't paying attention.

"Hey, let go," said Joseph, and she finally turned him loose. "What was that for?"

"Youssef Nissan," said Shahla. "You arrogant, mean, self-centered . . ."

"Hey, hey," interrupted Joseph. "Take it easy. I didn't mean it like it came out. I would have explained, but she just ran off."

"So she outran you?" asked Shahla. "Mr. Football?"

"I'll apologize," said Joseph. "But it was inappropriate. Girls don't ask guys to . . ."

"Don't you *even* start that macho crap with me, Youssef. Do you have any idea how scary it is to be alone in a place where you don't speak the language or know anyone . . . ?"

"Alright, alright. I'll go apologize," said Joseph, and he turned to the reception room door.

"It's too late," said Shahla. "They're gone. I was going to give her my mailing address so that she could write me, but she was crying, so her baba and maman took her back to their hotel. Our uncles had already asked them a hundred nosy questions. Good job, Youssef. Very appropriate Torah portion for you. Jerk."

Joseph sucked in his breath. "And die" was the difficult phrase of his Torah reading. He'd killed the sad girl with four words so he could get back to his party. And Shahla had used the worst insult in her limited vocabulary of insults. *Jerk.* That was a first time she'd ever called him one. He looked down. "Sorry," he said.

"I'm sorry, too," said Shahla. "Sorry I introduced her to you. She was so impressed at how well you sang, and she thought you were so handsome. Just goes to show that people aren't who you think they are."

Fereshteh thought he was handsome?

"Not a great way to treat a Jewish girl, Youssef," said Shahla. "Or any girl. It's not like she asked you to marry her. Just be a pen pal."

"I'm sorry, Shahla," said Joseph. "Really, I am."

Shahla searched his face. Joseph knew she'd forgive him, but she shrugged and left him standing there.

Back at the apartment, conversation with Shahla died once Baba and Maman retired for an afternoon nap. Shahla fell asleep on the couch. That left Joseph alone to think about the day. He swung back and forth between shame over what he'd said to Fereshteh and resentment for her ruining the perfection of his bar mitzvah. It was a quiet end to a noisy day.

20

CROWN JEWELS

Joseph was still thinking about Fereshteh when he and Baba walked to the synagogue for Yom Kippur prayers. Once he'd said the prayers of repentance, he felt better. Admitting what he'd done to God was like using an eraser on a chalkboard. Joseph could still faintly see the mistake beneath, but it was possible to write something new and better in its place.

Joseph tried to speed the walk to the apartment the evening after the last service of Yom Kippur, but Baba's steps remained as steady as always. Maman and Shahla had left the synagogue a little earlier. They had a light meal prepared when Joseph and Baba returned. At the apartment, Shahla lay on the sofa with her head in Maman's lap. Maman ran her fingers through Shahla's long, curly black hair. One of them had loosened it from its more severe, Yom Kippur–worthy formal chignon. The black curls draped in Maman's lap. They looked relaxed, at ease with one another.

Joseph stared at all the greeting cards and gifts stacked on the table. Now that Shabbat and Yom Kippur were over, he'd find out what his parents had given him. At Baba's gesture, they all moved to the table. First, Joseph opened Shahla's present of signed Astros caps, but she'd nestled a small flat box inside the bigger one. Inside the small box was a fine black leather wallet. Joseph rarely had more than a pocketful of chump change, but maybe the stack of gift cards included some cash to fill a real wallet. Just to be sure, Joseph thumbed open the wallet to see if there was money inside.

"Youssef!" Maman said, but Shahla laughed at his audacity. Joseph gave her cheek kisses to thank her, and he could see in her jade-green eyes he was forgiven.

"I have news," Baba said once he'd made the blessing over the meal. "My company is paying for me to take flying lessons to obtain my pilot's license. After that, I can use a company aircraft to fly to my jobs. I can finish site inspections faster and be home more."

Joseph snapped to full attention. He loved flying. His dresser was filled with model planes.

"I've decided to pay the instructor for you to learn, too, Joseph. You want to be a pilot, but you will be a *mehandes*, an engineer. You can design the planes and make a lot of money. The manufacturers are in cities where you can live in a Jewish community. It will not be so difficult to keep Shabbat and to find kosher food. It will help if you can actually fly the machines you design, so we can learn together."

Joseph wasn't sure how to do a cartwheel, but his heart did. Although Maman didn't hide her unease, Joseph could tell Baba had already talked to her about it. Joseph wanted to jump high and touch the ceiling like he did sometimes when he felt good.

He settled for smiling his toothiest grin since Baba signed the football release form.

Baba pointed to the biggest gift on the table, one that had appeared while they were at the synagogue praying. It was a big square box wrapped in brown paper. "That is your second gift. The first part of it anyway. The second part is ordered. You're growing so fast that it was hard to fit you."

What in the world could that be? Shahla grinned, so she already knew.

Joseph tore the paper away from the box. Inside was a sapphire-blue motorcycle helmet trimmed in white. "Wow, thank you for the helmet!" he said. Maybe they'd back-ordered gloves or boots. His feet were about the size of LaLa's Buick sedan.

"Remember when I took you to the mall to have you measured for your bar mitzvah suit?" asked Maman.

"Yes, ma'am." That had been a funny-in-Farsi adventure for Shahla.

"Your baba wanted your leg measurements. You're grow-ing so fast."

Joseph knew it. Custom riding boots like a motocross racer.

Baba handed Joseph a brochure from the shop where Mr. Ybarra repaired dirt bikes. Baba said, "We ordered you a new dirt bike. It will arrive with the next shipment."

Joseph opened the brochure and caught his breath. A new dirt bike? Flying lessons? This was beyond anything he could have thought to ask for. He'd have been glad to get a used dirt bike or just to have gone flying with Baba.

"No more piano playing, Youssef," said Baba. "These are gifts to teach you responsibility. No more excuses."

Shahla's face mirrored Joseph's disappointment at the prohibition against the piano, but she didn't have flying lessons and a dirt bike to distract her. Joseph wasn't really that worried that Baba would make him stop playing the piano completely.

21

THE DROP OF A HAT

It was their first Sunday-night phone call since his bar mitzvah.

"What's the latest?" asked Shahla.

"A mystery," said Joseph.

"That sounds intriguing," said Shahla. "What's the mystery?"

"I can't figure out why Maman and Baba didn't adopt you when your parents were killed. I know Maman loves you like a daughter. She says it evens the score when you're around. You don't let me get away with anything."

Shahla didn't say anything for several precious, long-distance seconds. She finally said, "I let you get away with all sorts of things."

"You know what I mean," said Joseph. "Serious things."

Shahla wasted more seconds.

"So do you have any idea?" asked Joseph. "You're older. Maybe you heard something."

"Yes."

"Yes, what?"

"Yes, I heard something."

"What did you hear?" asked Joseph. "You're burning time."

"Burning time," said Shahla vacantly. "That one would turn Maman inside out. I'll have to move the matches away from the clock."

"Sorry," said Joseph. "I wasn't thinking." Shahla's parents had burned in a car bomb. That was stupid of him not to think of that. After all, he was reminding her that she'd been left behind . . . twice. Her parents had left her with babysitters when they went to Israel, and Joseph's parents had left her behind when they left California. Joseph was too young to remember when they moved to Texas, but by his calculation, they left California right after the bombing.

"It's okay," said Shahla. "My parents told me that the family didn't think it was safe for me to go with Aunt Miriam. There was trouble in Iran. It affected both our families. Your baba said that if we split up, then it would be safer for me."

"Safer?" asked Joseph. "We're together in the summers and holidays. How is that safer?"

"I don't know, Youssef."

Joseph could hear the deep rejection in the softness of her answer. Should he press on and keep hurting her, or stop and try something more upbeat?

"I love my parents, Youssef. Don't feel sorry for me," said Shahla, this time with resolution. "They're my real parents. I'm grateful they are from Iran and speak Farsi. I would have flunked kindergarten if Baba hadn't given me a crash course in English."

She was completely loyal to her adoptive parents, Joseph had to hand her that. Better to stop the conversation before he insulted the only parents she really remembered. He had more information to go on now. *Safer.* That word kept coming up. Who in Iran could be after his family? Was the car bomb not a random act?

Joseph heard Maman's footsteps approaching the kitchen. "Maman's coming. Quick, what am I thinking?"

But there was only a click. Shahla had hung up.

Yeah, he wasn't thinking.

22

CAP FUNDS

LaLa was never one to waste words. Now that Baba's invisible eye scrutinized Joseph's time with her, Joseph didn't waste words, either. Baba allowed Joseph to check on her each day, but football practice and homework took so much time that he only had a bit of time to say hello, maybe plunk around on the piano to try out some song he'd heard on the radio. Not long, or he was afraid Baba would find out and stop the flying lessons.

It was in his attempt at the Eagles' "Wasted Time" that LaLa informed him of his new voice. Joseph was trying his best to imitate Don Henley. In the short time between Miss LaNell's favorite orchid song and now, his voice had changed. "You're a baritone now, Joseph," she said.

"Really?" asked Joseph. That made him feel good. He'd be tall like Baba, and he didn't want to sound like Michael Jackson.

"Yes," said LaLa. "You have that raspy, blues edge. You'll drive the girls crazy."

Not much chance of that. Baba would have a fit if he played

the piano in public. It was cool that he could sound like Don Henley, though. LaLa went to the kitchen, and Joseph tried it again. He knew he'd nailed it because he heard a little knock on the kitchen table. That was how LaLa signaled her approval of a piece, one little knock on whatever surface was available. Joseph grinned to himself and went to the kitchen.

"Come have a snack," said LaLa. "I kept a package of Little Debbies for you."

When Joseph told LaLa about the flying lessons and the dirt bike, she gave him a sad smile. "You're leaving me, dear," she said.

"Leaving you? How?" asked Joseph.

"Wings, wheels, cleats . . . you're growing up and moving on. Rolling and flying away as young folks do. In another year or two, you'll come to see me even less. Eventually you'll just wave if you see me in the yard or come check on me after a storm. That's the way of life with young men."

"LaLa, that's not true. I've been here almost every day since I was in first grade."

"It will happen, Joseph, and I want you to remember this moment. Right here, right now, you have my permission to grow up . . ."

"No, LaLa," interrupted Joseph, his heart lurching. "You need me. I take care of you so Mr. Thaddeus can rest easy."

LaLa smiled that red-lipstick smile. "I know I told you that, dear, but Mr. Thaddeus will rest just as easy when you go. In fact, I'm sure that when you step away, it will bring Mr. Thaddeus and me a step closer to that waltz he loves so much. Just don't you feel bad, dear, when you're sixteen or eighteen or twenty-one, and you think about me or see me, and worry. I'll understand, and it's the way of men and women. Some things have to end before new things begin. The world runs in its cycles. Mr. Kamran is right to teach you and provide you the opportunities to become a fine man."

"He's just backward, LaLa," said Joseph. "But he'll come around and let me start spending more time with you after flying lessons on Sunday. It's only that I think he was scared Reverend Baer would call the police. It's silly to be afraid of police."

"Don't begrudge your father and mother their burdens, Joseph. And don't become one of them."

———

Baba carefully read the newspaper headlines each morning when he was home, and he saved every paper. In the evenings and weekends, he read every word in the world, politics, and financial sections. Relatives sometimes sent Farsi-language news articles, and Baba and Maman discussed them. What did the political changes in Iran mean? It was very personal to them.

Two weeks after his bar mitzvah, Baba and Maman arranged to go early in the day to Dallas. Joseph received over six hundred dollars in cash and checks for bar mitzvah gifts. Baba let Joseph choose the amount he'd give to charity. He gave him twenty-five dollars to spend on whatever he wanted. That left five hundred dollars, which Baba put in a little safe in his office. It was easy to spend the coins Maman gave him each morning. Now that he had his own money, Joseph put the bills in his new wallet and guarded them zealously.

Today, Baba had Joseph's cash envelope along with his own briefcase when they got in the car to drive to Dallas. This was curious, but Baba only said that Joseph would find out more when they got there. "There" was some kind of office in Dallas. It wasn't like the local banks in Hazel, which were First and Second National Banks, like the First and Second Baptist Churches. Joseph never could figure out why you'd name anything "Second" unless it was a street. Baba wanted Joseph to invest his money. That's why they had to go to this special office.

Baba checked in with the secretary, and they waited in the reception area. Maman sat, but Baba took Joseph over to a wall that had a huge poster of the United States. There were little stars marking the cities where the institution had offices. "Memorize this, Youssef," said Baba, pointing to the major cities. "I want you to remember where you can withdraw money if you need to."

How weird. Why wouldn't Joseph just come here if he needed the money?

They were ushered back to the financial agent's office. Baba introduced Joseph to the agent. "Joseph wants to invest his bar mitzvah money in the stock market," said Baba to the agent.

Well, thanks for asking, Baba. It had never crossed Joseph's mind to invest in the stock market. Whatever that was. He kind of remembered something from social studies class about people jumping out of windows when the stock market crashed. It was a good thing they lived in a single-story house. Joseph already knew he'd survive a jump from his bedroom window. It was climbing back in that was a problem.

Baba placed the envelope with five hundred dollars cash on the agent's desk. What followed was lots of explanations about high- and low-risk funds, bonds, rates of return, and long-term planning for college expenses. "I'm going to get a football scholarship," said Joseph. "I don't need college money."

That made the agent grin, but not Baba. "You're going to engineering school, Joseph," said Baba. "Not playing games for college."

"No, Baba, the football scholarship pays for the tuition. I can still go to engineering school at the same time."

Baba gave him the look that said to cool it because they were in front of a stranger. Maman patted him on the leg and said in Farsi, "No matter what happens in life, you need money to get by. You never know when something bad will happen."

Joseph glumly moved his eyes back to the pamphlets spread out on the agent's desk. In the end, Baba signed papers on his behalf because he was a minor. The secretary came in and used a funny round stamp on everything. All that was left of the five hundred dollars cash was a nicely written receipt. It did feel nice when the agent gave him a business card along with a handful of pamphlets explaining what he had just invested in. The thick pamphlets and sheaf of papers made no sense, but it felt very grown-up. The secretary brought in cold Cokes and a bowl of assorted candies. Most of it was kosher. Oh, yeah. Sweet, sweet. And the business card slid right in one of the little slots for credit cards in his wallet.

After Joseph's account was set up, Baba handed the agent a bank check to deposit into his own account. While the agent processed the deposit and went over Baba's last year of earnings, Joseph drank Maman's Coke and picked through the candy bowl for the Brach's butterscotch and miniature Hershey ones. He'd have to check with the other boys at the synagogue to see if their dads made them invest their bar mitzvah money.

The agent and Baba wrapped it up, and they went back out through the reception area. Baba took Joseph by the arm and led him once again to the big map. Baba was tall enough to reach to the top of the map. His long index finger traced down the East Coast, drawing circles around New York, Boston, and Washington, DC. "Remember these locations, Youssef. There are international airports with flights to Israel in these cities."

Joseph nodded and scooped out a few more butterscotch and Hershey candies from another bowl that sat on the counter. Right. Airports and money. Got it.

23
STRAW HAT

Joseph placed the change in the lunch cashier's hand for the chocolate milk and went to the condiment counter to find a straw. He hated drinking milk straight from the carton. He checked the three lunch lines. Roberto, Mateo, and the rest of the gang were still shuffling inch by inch through the heavy aroma of the tomato sauce that hung over the cafeteria every day except Friday, which was hamburger day. Mateo said that they used the same tasteless sauce for spaghetti, pizza, meatloaf, and meatball hoagies. In that case, thought Joseph, it wasn't so bad to bring a kosher sack lunch.

Joseph scanned the lunchroom for a table with room for their group, but their usual table was mostly full. Across the room, Joseph spotted Vonda sitting at a table with her girl-friends. The seat next to her was open.

Why not?

Joseph sat down next to her. The looks from the girls were all inside jokes and smirky smiles, like when the coaches let the boys and girls use the gym together on rainy days. "Is this okay?" asked Joseph.

"Sure," said Vonda. She looked genuinely happy to see him.

"Privacy?" she suggested to the table. They threw one another those strange, feminine looks, but they picked up their trays and moved down.

Joseph removed his requested peanut butter and jelly sandwich, glad that Maman hadn't packed a container of *dolmeh*. Texans were big on turnip greens, but they'd probably never rolled anything up in grape leaves. They chatted a few minutes, and then Vonda put her hand on the table like she was going to say something important.

"I'm sorry," said Vonda. "For what my father said."

"I didn't really understand it," said Joseph.

"You know? I really didn't either," said Vonda.

They both smiled. It wasn't something to laugh about, but a smile worked.

"I miss your hat," she said. "It was different. It made you look very dressed up."

Joseph took a bite of his sandwich. "Yeah, well, in this town, I'm more likely to get beat up when I dress up, so I don't . . ." He let the sentence trail off. "Oh, guess what?" he said, making sure his tone was upbeat. You never saw pretty girls hanging around sad dudes, only confident ones.

"What?"

"I'm playing football now."

"I know. I saw you standing with the team at the last few pep rallies. Do you like it?"

She had noticed him in his jersey! Joseph tried to stay cool. "Yeah, Coach says if I keep improving, I might be able to move up to first-string by the end of the season."

"Nissan!"

Joseph looked around, and Roberto was standing next to a table a few rows over, beckoning to him. Joseph stared back, frowning. Roberto moved his eyes to Vonda and then back to Joseph. Mateo looked, too, and then he said something to Roberto. Roberto said something back that made the whole group laugh. They sat, and Joseph turned back to Vonda.

"They call you Nissan?" said Vonda.

"Yeah. The coaches call me Nissan, so they started calling me Nissan to tease me about playing football, I guess."

"Does anyone ever call you Joe?" she asked.

"Joe?"

"Instead of Joseph," Vonda said. "You know, like a nickname."

"You can call me anything you want," said Joseph. *Except Jewish Boy.*

"But no one's ever called you Joe?" she persisted.

"No."

Vonda took his hand, and it thrilled him like the first time. This time she examined his long fingers, seeming to admire them. She glanced up at his face. "I can see why. You're too dignified. You don't drink straight out of the milk carton like the rest of the boys. I still see you dressed up like at Miss Eleanor's even though now you're wearing jeans."

She'd noticed his jeans? Emmmm . . .

24
SHOWER CAP

It wasn't hard to do. Joseph invited Vonda and her friends into their lunch table group. Even though he made rounds through the cafeteria frequently to chat with other students or went to work on student council business, even Mateo liked the new company. A vote was a vote. Mateo would make a good politician someday. He already was. He'd prevented a cafeteria boycott when the administration decided to remove the soda machines from the cafeteria so students would make "healthier choices." With Mateo's negotiation, the soda machines were installed in the outside courtyard, and the cafeteria funds remained healthy.

Everyone at school began to assume Vonda was Joseph's girlfriend. From their regular date at lunch, Joseph walked her to fifth period class. Because their classrooms were close by, he walked her from second to third period. They didn't hold hands, but Joseph did work up the courage occasionally to walk with his hand protectively in the small of her back. That was it, though. Joseph couldn't call Vonda at night. Baba would have a fit in Farsi if Joseph were caught talking to a girl, especially Reverend Charles Baer's daughter.

The arrangement suited Vonda. Joseph was sure she feared her father's wrath way more than he feared Baba's. It was on the long Shabbats that Joseph thought about Vonda a lot. Football practice after school and games kept him busy and tired through the week.

It was the solid crack of shoulder pads colliding that Joseph loved at football practice. He especially liked the sound of his own pads connecting with a runner's. It was more personal than dodgeball. The first two weeks of contact practice, he came home sore and hardly able to move every night. He'd been so sore that he declined the Monday-night boxing class. Baba decided to suspend boxing until after football season.

The coaches tried to put Joseph with the receivers in practice. He was fast despite his height. It made sense because he caught the throws from the quarterback easily. Once he understood the mechanics of the game, Joseph saw that his build suited the position of tight end. He didn't want to play that position, though. He wanted to play defense.

"Why?" asked the coach when Joseph asked him the third time to put him on defense. "Don't you want to make touchdowns?"

"I want to hit." *And I don't want to catch anything thrown by an Edmondson.*

"You can hit the defense. Block for the offense."

"No, I want to hit hard. I don't want to be tackled."

"Son," said the coach. "This is football. You'll be tackled one way or the other."

"I know. But I want to play defense."

The coach growled something about kids not being grateful, but he let Joseph practice with both the offensive and defensive units. On Sundays after flying lessons, Joseph watched an hour of professional football on LaLa's television. He studied the tackling methods and tried to understand offensive and defensive formations. Occasionally Baba would come sit with him, and Joseph explained the game. When you knew a little about something, you were the expert to someone who knew nothing. Baba pretended to be interested, but he'd soon doze in the chair, long fingers draped over the armrest.

Football was the state religion of Texas. If Joseph could be good at it, then it was what Baba had talked about: do something better than anyone else. There was another reason Joseph wanted to hit. Baba had said Joseph couldn't do anything to make someone call the police. But what if he could hit someone legally? If he could receive recognition instead of a belt-whipping, like the one that had so stripped his dignity after the fight at Rehkopf's?

Larry Edmondson was the cat-eyed grimy boy. His sidekick was Brian. Larry was the eighth-grade starting quarterback. Brian was a second-string running back. Both played on offense. If Joseph played defense, he would have opportunities . . . a responsibility . . . to tackle them in practice. Hard.

What made Joseph hate them even more was how the Edmondsons pretended to pal around with their Hispanic teammates. As if playing football made a Hispanic a useful pet. The Edmondsons didn't know a *gato* from a *perro*.

Juan Garza was huge. The high school coaches already drooled over him. He was six foot two in eighth grade, a chunk of muscle shaped by working with his father, who was the foreman of a local ranch. Mr. Ybarra and Mr. Garza were friends.

Joseph had met Juan at Mr. Ybarra's place when he was with Mateo and Roberto riding dirt bikes.

Juan played center. He hiked the ball to Larry, and then he protected him while Larry passed, handed off, or ran with the ball. Everybody liked Juan. You had to. Not because he was so big, but because he was so courteous. A gentle giant. Even if he smashed a defender, he always helped him up after the whistle blew. Coach Meeks had little tantrums, saying that football was a war, not a dance, and Juan should never help up a player on defense. Juan would nod seriously and say, "Yes, sir." He'd do it on the very next play.

Joseph found out why Juan helped up defensive players, though. When he was on the receiving end of Juan's smashing blocks in practice, Juan helped him up with a smile and said softly, "Don't bring that garbage my way, Skinny Boy. You gonna get hurt." It made you think.

Larry strutted around the locker room and called Juan his personal Rottweiler. Toughest dog in Texas. Juan never reacted to Larry's boasting. Joseph wondered if Juan knew how the Edmondsons really felt about him. Juan was friendly, but never talkative. It was hard to tell if he liked it or merely tolerated it like a Rottweiler tolerated a yapping little mutt. It was Juan, however, who stopped Brian's bullying in the locker room.

Brian pulled Joseph's towel off and wolf-whistled at him when he came out of the showers. That was it. Naked or not, police or not, Joseph was going to fight him again or die trying. Before he could chase Brian down the locker room bench row, a huge body moved between them. Juan Garza hooked Brian's shoulder with an enormous paw, spinning him around on the damp floor.

Brian started to say something, but his eyes widened. He started slowly sinking. Juan held him along the collarbone, but he was somehow squeezing . . . and squeezing . . . and squeezing. It looked paralyzing, and Brian sank to his knees, mouth open and face screwed up in pain.

"You don' do that to him no more," said Juan.

Brian's mouth formed an O. It opened and closed like a guppy's.

Larry looked on from a bench the next row over, but he didn't say anything. Joseph wrapped the towel back around himself.

"You don' call him names no more," added Juan.

More fish gupping.

"You leave him alone. He's still jus' a little kid. He don' bother you none."

Tears started streaming down Brian's thin cheeks.

"We good, now, dude?" asked Juan patiently. "Or I gotta 'splain it to you again?"

Brian nodded, then shook his head vigorously.

"Okay." Juan released his grip. "You remember our little talk next time I block for you, right?" He said it loud enough that it carried to the next row. For that matter, the whole locker room heard. You could hear a pin drop even over the water splatter in the showers.

Brian nodded. And Larry said nothing. A center who wouldn't block made the quarterback and running backs fresh meat to the defense. Juan rarely had occasion to block for Brian. He blocked every play for Larry.

"You okay, little guy?" Juan asked Joseph. Joseph was one of the tallest on the eighth-grade team, but next to Juan, he was just a little guy. Juan had more body hair than Baba.

The locker room fell to a low murmur, and Brian practically skipped down the aisle to get dressed.

"I'm okay," said Joseph. "*Estoy bien. Gracias.*"

"Mateo said you a good guy. Mateo gonna be mayor of this town someday," said Juan matter-of-factly, as if it were something as sure as the sun coming up in the morning. "He gonna be the governor of Texas maybe."

"I sure hope so," said Joseph. "But I'd vote for you, too."

And that was the end of the Edmondson problem at school. Anywhere. The word was out. Sometimes the other players called him Skinny Boy, and a few of the players still called him Pretty Boy, but it was more of the guy-to-guy tease. It meant Joseph was part of the team family, especially as his tackling improved. He wasn't just the kid who was freaky good at math, the walking-stick answer key to homework. Muscle memory made Joseph's hits better and better. Tackling hard was the same as punching hard in boxing class. It was a matter of estimating where you wanted the punch to land and timing according to the opponent's movements.

Now Joseph knew how to make things even for LaLa's ruined groceries. All Joseph had to do was convince Juan to have a bad series of downs on offense.

25
HAT STAND

Joseph started with Brian. That's why Joseph was moved up to first-string. Brian wasn't that big, and he wasn't that fast, but he hit the line of scrimmage with his short legs pumping. Brian could squirt through the defense because they didn't hit him low enough. That was probably how he had made the team.

Any time Brian ran the ball, Joseph paid special attention, trying to learn his habits. The good news was that the second-string offensive line wasn't that great. They didn't give Brian much protection. There was a world of difference and a ton of body hair that separated the second-string offensive line and Juan Garza. And that was Joseph's opportunity. He waited. He stalked. When the day came that they scrimmaged in full pads, the third-down play call was the green light.

Joseph read the play. Brian always rubbed his palms on the fronts of his thigh pads when it was a pass. The quarterback faked a handoff, but he tossed a little play-action pass to Brian, who caught it. Joseph gunned off the line of scrimmage, driving hard, connecting with Brian just as the football brushed Brian's fingers. There was a satisfying crack, and Brian fell and lay still. Joseph rolled up to his feet victoriously. He'd made the tackle behind the line of scrimmage.

Brian didn't move. He lay there like Texas roadkill. Bring the shovel, boys. Possum on the pavement.

Everything on the field went quiet. Even the first-string stopped their drills to turn and look. The offensive and defensive assistant coaches walked toward Brian, who finally tried to raise his head. Both coaches knelt and talked to him. One coach unsnapped his helmet. They stayed there for a few minutes, and then the coaches took Brian's arms and helped him to his feet. The offensive coach waved in another running back. Brian had just found out it was a war, not a dance. The coaches didn't have to worry about Joseph wanting to help Brian to his feet.

Coach Meeks was the head coach, and he walked from the other side of the field where the first-string players were running drills. He talked to Brian for a minute. Satisfied that Brian's minimal IQ was undamaged, he talked to the defensive coach for a minute. The other players took the opportunity to take off their helmets and let the fall breeze cool their faces. The coaches kept looking toward Joseph. Was he in trouble?

Finally, Coach Meeks turned back to the other side of the field. He motioned to Joseph. "Nissan, come with me."

Joseph snapped his chin strap back on and trotted after him to the other end of the field where first-string was running drills. First-string would scrimmage the next day in full pads. Okay. One down, one to go. Larry glanced at Joseph a few times in the drills, but other than that, he said nothing. In the locker room, Larry didn't say anything either. Brian was already gone. Juan patted Joseph on the head to say congratulations. Joseph breathed a sigh of relief. If the Edmondsons jumped him, it wouldn't be in the locker room. Larry had his pet dog story backward.

Brian wasn't really gone, though. As Joseph and a couple of other boys rounded the back corner of the gym to go to the bike racks, Joseph saw Brian hand an older boy something. The boy handed something back. The other boy looked like he was probably a junior or senior in high school. Larry stood about thirty feet away, watching toward the sidewalk to the front of the building, the main approach to the gym. If he wasn't going to get his bicycle, what was Brian doing back here? And why was Larry watching for him?

"Man, those guys are gonna get in so much trouble," said the boy next to Joseph.

"What are they doing?" asked Joseph.

"Brian sells pot. You didn't know that?"

"Nah," said Joseph. "Not my crowd. My dad would kill me."

"Yeah, mine, too," said the boy.

Larry gave Joseph a glance, but he was preoccupied with whatever he was looking for. Joseph guessed that Larry was supposed to warn Brian if an adult came up the walk toward the gym.

The next day, Joseph dressed out knowing that he'd be scrimmaging with the first-string team. The starters. Taking out Brian wasn't too hard, but Brian was smaller than Larry, and he didn't have Juan Garza protecting him on the line. Joseph hadn't noticed Larry having any giveaway habits, either. Joseph would have to read the offense and be fast off the line when he thought it was a pass. When it came down to it, he didn't want to ask Juan to let him by on a pass rush. Joseph wanted to flatten Larry all on his own.

The practice was nearly over before Joseph had his chance. He'd thought Larry didn't have any giveaway habits, but he did notice the slightest change in the pitch and cadence of Larry's voice on a pass play. Joseph worked hard to master the cantillation marks when he'd prepared for his bar mitzvah. His ear was well-tuned. That was another way he had of frustrating LaLa. He could hear a tune and play it by ear, so she was never sure if he was imitating the notes or reading the music.

Joseph played defensive end, the exact spot he'd begged for. Practiced for. In boxing class, Joseph learned it was important to relax, to shake his muscles loose before unleashing a strong attack. Joseph rolled his shoulders and neck as Larry moved up to the line of scrimmage. When Larry crouched behind Juan's big butt to call the play, Joseph levered down, too. He forced his abdomen down to breathe in the maximum amount of oxygen.

Although the sky was overcast, for a moment everything was clear and bright. The blades of dry, brown grass beneath Joseph's fingers weren't soft, yet they were pliable. Another deep breath, and the odor of stale perspiration from his helmet mingled with the fresh air. A tickling trickle of sweat worked its way from beneath his pads and slid into the small of his back. In the clarity of perfect control, Joseph heard it. Larry's voice pitched slightly higher, and there was the briefest hesitation as he called the count.

When Juan's fingers tightened on the ball, Joseph teed off the line of scrimmage and went straight for Larry like a guided missile. He was through the offensive line before they could even react. Juan never had a chance to backpedal far enough to protect Larry. Joseph hit him with everything he had. Larry's head snapped, and the ball slipped out of his hands before he could get it past chest level. Larry was bigger than Brian, and Joseph had to drive his legs hard. He carried Larry a few yards into the backfield before they fell together.

"Get off me, you greaser son of a bitch," said Larry raggedly. Joseph had taken him down hard enough to knock a lot of the wind out of him. Sweet.

"I'm not Mexican," said Joseph, intentionally delaying, keeping Larry pinned to the ground. "You need to work on your football skills and your geography skills."

"You're not Mexican?" asked Larry.

Joseph affected a Texas drawl and put his face mask close to Larry's: "Ain't that somethin'?"

"*Nissan!*"

Oy veh.

Coach Meeks slammed down his clipboard, grabbed Joseph by the back of the shoulder pads, and pulled him off Larry. The coach twirled Joseph around, pushed him hard, and then reeled him back in by grabbing his face mask. "Don't you ever, *ever*, hit your own quarterback like that again! You understand me, son? Are you clear?" He pressed his face right up into Joseph's face mask, and little bubbles of spit came out one side of his mouth. "'Cause I can make it really, really clear to you."

So much for it being a war and not a dance.

Coach Meeks ranted, "Do you not see that red vest over his jersey? It means you don't tackle him hard. Do you know how hard it is to replace a quarterback?"

"Yes, sir," said Joseph. Good grief.

Juan helped Larry to his feet. Maybe he hadn't heard the greaser comment.

Or maybe he had.

Larry's offensive line got the next butt chewing. They were invited to run the bleachers with Joseph after practice. That would make him popular in the locker room. He'd get a few wet towel snaps on his butt for that. When Coach Meeks was done having a fit, he took a deep breath and picked up his clipboard. "Nissan."

"Yes, sir."

"You're starting at defensive end on Thursday. If you hit their quarterback as hard as you hit Edmondson, you've got the job permanently."

26

HARD HAT

Baba and Maman came to watch Joseph's first home game as a starter. Baba was working out of the local office that week, and he talked her into it. Maman heard Joseph try to explain the football games to Baba, and she'd shake her head. Joseph reassured her that it wasn't as violent as it sounded. After a bit of negotiation, she agreed to go. The Hawks were playing the first-place team in their division Thursday night.

Joseph kept searching the stands during the pregame warm-ups. He finally spotted his parents in the visitors bleachers. They must have been attracted to the extra room. On the home side, the band, pep squad, and spectators packed the stands. It took several tries, but Joseph finally got his parents' attention. He pointed them to the home bleachers. For the next five minutes, each time he looked their way, he could see them discussing the problem. It was Maman who kept pointing to the Hawks' black-and-gold jerseys, the black-and-gold band uniforms, pep squad uniforms, and cheerleaders' uniforms. She was trying to get Baba to see that they should sit where all the colors matched.

The teams finished warm-ups and gathered at the ends of the field for their pep talks. Joseph continued glancing around to see where Baba and Maman were. They disappeared from the visitors side, so maybe Maman's common sense prevailed over Baba's engineering for extra space. He finally spotted them in the home bleachers. In the cool weather, Maman's head scarf didn't stand out so much.

From time to time, Joseph checked the stands. Baba and Maman sat stoically amid the screaming, pom-pom waving, stomping, and groaning going on around them. Baba was trying to look anywhere to avoid the cheerleaders' barelegged prancing and bobbing. Joseph knew from experience that it wasn't easy to do, but then again, he'd never tried not to. Maman periodically pointed at Joseph, probably trying to connect the number on the black jersey to her son. Baba nodded solemnly.

The game was still tied at 3–3 with only three minutes left in the fourth quarter. Even Juan was unable to penetrate the offensive line so that the Hawks' running backs could gain much yardage. The two sacks in the first quarter proved that Larry wouldn't find much in the way of passing. Joseph did well tackling. He especially liked it when he heard his name over the PA for making or assisting on a tackle. The guy calling the game mispronounced Nissan, but that was okay.

Joseph was standing on the sideline squirting Gatorade into his mouth when he heard his name. "Nissan!"

This time the man saying his name pronounced it correctly. It was Coach Meeks. "Yes, sir," said Joseph, shouldering his way through the other boys on the sideline. Yo front and center.

"You remember your blocking assignments at tight end?"

"Yes, sir."

The coach inclined his head to the opposing defensive back who had just stuffed the Hawks' running back at the line of scrimmage . . . again. It was number forty-six, the defensive back who'd been wrecking Larry's offense the whole game. Coach Meeks said, "You're reporting as an offensive player. I want you to block number forty-six. We're running the play his way. Put everything you have into it. Keep it legal, keep it safe, but hit him. Textbook. You understand?"

"Yes, sir."

The coach gave him the play to carry to Larry. Joseph snapped on his chin strap and trotted onto the field, jerking his thumb to let the tight end know he was out and Joseph was in. Larry looked up at him in the huddle, and Joseph gave him the play. "We're running at him *again*?" asked Larry.

"Yeah," said Joseph.

Larry held Joseph's eyes for a long moment. Joseph knew that Larry didn't really think Joseph was going to protect him. Larry thought he was about to get bulldozed again by number forty-six. It was a delicious hopelessness for Joseph to see, like peach sharbet melting on pavement. Juan just stood there with sweat dripping from the end of his nose as steady as a faucet. He was exhausted. Juan wasn't really built for stamina. Well, he wasn't built for speed, either. He was built for strength, and it looked like he'd reached the end of it.

Larry called the play, though, and they said, "Ready . . . break!" with a clap.

Joseph didn't practice much on offense, but he knew what to do. Larry was running the ball. Joseph was supposed to block anyone who got in Larry's way, but he hoped it was number forty-six. If he missed his block, then number forty-six would flatten Larry like a steamroller. The number forty-six kid was some kind of early-maturing freak, much heavier and faster than Joseph or Larry.

Larry crouched under Juan.

Rage. Control.

"Blue-44. Blue-44. Set . . . hut, hut!" Larry took the snap and ran right. Here came number forty-six like a cannonball. Joseph drew a bead on him, put his shoulder down, and hit him just like Coach said, textbook. At those speeds, though, a textbook block made their pads *smack-crack* together mightily.

Both number forty-six and Joseph went to the ground, and both crawled to their knees slowly. Meanwhile, Joseph heard the home bleachers erupt. He looked down the field. Larry had gained thirty-two yards on the run before their safety ran him out of bounds. First down. The band played a rousing tribute, and Larry was grinning when he came back to the huddle. He didn't say thanks, but Joseph didn't expect him to. They were both doing their jobs. Larry had just better not call Joseph his personal Rottweiler. Joseph looked to the sideline, expecting to be waved back out, but a receiver ran to the huddle with the next play. This time, Larry was supposed to pass to Joseph.

Joseph had never caught a pass in a game, only in practice. Maybe Larry saw the doubt in Joseph's eyes. "You can do it, kid," said Larry. "Piece of cake."

Yeah, and if Larry hadn't ruined LaLa's bag of groceries, there would have been a piece of cake. The bitterness of the memory brought some determination. Joseph nodded.

Larry's pass over the middle was perfect. Joseph caught it on the fly. All he could think of was "textbook," so he tucked away the ball carefully and ran where he saw space. He was bumped with missed tackles a couple of times, but he wasn't pulled down until he'd gained nineteen yards. Now they were in scoring position. The band burst into another slightly off-key tribute to his gaining another first down.

Joseph looked up. Baba and Maman stood with everyone else in the home bleachers. They didn't look sure why they were glad that their son was dragged into the grass, but they were glad nonetheless. Maman had a little black-and-gold pom-pom on a stick. She waved it, glancing around to make sure she was doing the right thing. That made Joseph grin even more than his teammates smacking him on the back. If he could hear his parents' conversation in the bleachers, he could keep Shahla entertained for a month of Sunday-evening phone calls. This was quite a first for their record book, too.

The next play was a pass. Larry threw it perfectly. Joseph was winded, but he executed the block, and the Hawks' receiver caught the pass and ran it in for a touchdown. The home bleachers erupted again. This time the band played the full Hawks fight song. Coach Meeks gave Larry and Joseph happy butt slaps and a "Good job!" when they ran back to the sideline. The extra point was good.

Joseph looked into the stands. Baba smiled down at him while Maman waved her pom-pom. Could life get any better?

27
HAT DANCE

"Youssef, what is exactly dis eh-stuff?" Maman called.

Joseph hurriedly finished shaping his hair with a comb.
"What stuff?"

"Come, *Aziz-am.*"

Joseph checked his curls to make sure he didn't have any
rowdy ones messing up the new hairstyle he'd chosen for his
bar mitzvah. Baba took him to his own barber instead of letting
Maman's stylist savage Joseph's black mop. Maman had long
hair that she kept under a headscarf, so she only went now and
then to have it trimmed. As a result, Joseph's hair went from
short to long curls over a long cycle. Now he had a closer cut
on the sides and a shorter length on top. Vonda assured him he
looked very much like the guys in the style books at the beauty
shop. He planned to go with Baba to every barber visit to make
sure it stayed that way.

"Youssef!"

"Coming, Maman." Joseph hustled into the kitchen, not

sure what "dis eh-stuff" was. Hopefully she hadn't been digging through his school bag and found a jockstrap or a note from Vonda. Football season was over, and he was practicing with the basketball team. New sport, new equipment for his private parts, private being the key word.

His breakfast was laid out on the table, but it was the Dallas newspaper that she held out to him like a relay runner passing a baton. On the front page was a picture of the Shah of Iran stepping off a plane. Joseph read the first few paragraphs of the article while Maman crowded in. She scanned the English words, not trusting herself to understand them.

"The Shah of Iran came to America yesterday," said Joseph. "He's come for cancer treatment."

"No," said Maman. "He cannot come here."

"He can't?"

"No," said Maman. "He cannot come here. No, no, no." She slapped her hand on the breakfast table to emphasize each *no*. Joseph let one side of the paper go so he could grab the yogurt before it bounced off the table to the floor.

"Why, Maman?" What harm could it do for the Shah of Iran to come to the States for medical treatment? According to the papers, he'd already left Iran in the hands of the revolutionaries. The game was over. He was free to play tennis anywhere in the world.

"Dis man cannot come here," she said, using English as if it could ward off the fallen Iranian king. Joseph folded the paper to get the source of her agitation out of sight, but she snatched it away.

"I mus' eh-speak to your fader," said Maman. She went to the kitchen drawer that held her address book. The force with which she jerked open the drawer rattled everything inside.

Call Baba at work? When he was in the oil field? Unheard of. What was going on? Joseph's calm, unflappable mother had been replaced by an angry woman who danced from the countertop where she flipped through the address book to the phone on the wall and back again. She wouldn't put down the paper or the phone receiver. The phone was tethered too far from the kitchen counter for her to read the number. She paced back and forth until Joseph picked up the address book and followed her to the phone so she could dial.

When she finished dialing, Maman motioned him out of the kitchen. "You go to de school now, Youssef," she said.

"But I haven't eaten breakfast."

"You take and go."

"I don't have a spoon . . ."

Maman stretched the phone cord until it was taut, stacked his two pieces of peanut butter toast on top of the yogurt cup, and handed it to him. She picked up the spoon and stuck it in his front shirt pocket. "Now you have eh-spoon. Go to de school."

"You don't want me to talk to them for you?" asked Joseph. "Tell them who you are and who you need to contact?"

"No. You go now."

It bothered Joseph all day at school. He'd seen Maman anxious or frustrated, but never genuinely angry. This was far beyond even the Uncle Eli level of agitation. Joseph talked to Roberto and Alex about it in homeroom after Mr. Chappelle handed out the new school lunch menus and calendar. Neither Alex nor Roberto understood Iranian politics. Honestly, Joseph didn't either. He only knew that his parents had left Iran to escape the secret police, who must have worked for the Shah. The Shah was like a king or something.

"Go by the library," suggested Alex. "See if there are any books on Iran."

Joseph cut him a look, and Roberto said, "Nah, don't do that. Only a dumbass would read a book to find out about where his parents came from."

"That's not true," Alex objected. "I don't know the first thing about Mexico except everything's cheap, the food's good, and my grandmother makes really good tamales with the venison my grandfather and father bring back after they go hunting there. And the Mexican hat dance. And piñatas. And *The Love Boat* goes there. Other than that, I got nothing." After thinking a little more, he said, "I had to check out a book from the library on Mexico. I had to do a report on Santa Anna for Mrs. Draper's class. I don't plan to read another book until I have to do another book report."

"We're Mateo's worst nightmare," cracked Roberto. "Skinny Boy here don't know nothing 'bout Iran, you hate reading books on Mexico, and I don't read nothing but the lunch menu." The three of them laughed until Mr. Chappelle put his coffee down. There was no real danger he'd get off his stool, but that was the unwritten homeroom agreement. You didn't make Mr. Chappelle get off his stool, so he didn't get off his stool.

When Joseph got home from school, things were a little better. Maman was no longer agitated, but she was sullen. As it turned out, she was better at it than Joseph, and he thought he was pretty good. She'd calmed down, but nothing erased her resentment for the Shah's visit to America. Joseph wasn't home late from practice, but she scolded him. Maman closed the kitchen cabinet doors harder than necessary and shut the drawers too firmly. The phone rang a lot that night, too. Two calls from California and a middle-of-the-night call from Israel. Baba called back before bedtime.

Maman made Joseph leave the kitchen while she talked. He eavesdropped anyway. The one side of the conversations he could follow centered around the Shah's visit and whether his security team was with him. How long he might stay. Whether the Shah was moving to America permanently. Maman's accusation that whoever was on the other end had a hand in starting all the trouble. The distressing one was the offer for Maman and Joseph to come stay in Israel for a while.

Although Joseph heard her say no, that got his attention. Did Maman hate the Shah so badly that she didn't want to be in the same country with him? Or did the Shah's government still have some power that might harm them even here? It was impossible to sleep much that night. As the days passed, Maman's anxiety about it lessened, which relieved Joseph. He couldn't imagine moving to Israel now.

28

TIP OF THE HAT

"Hey," said Joseph. "Want me to walk you home from school?"

Vonda gave him that maddening look. It was impossible to tell whether she was pleased or only vaguely interested when he walked her to English class. "Don't you have your bicycle?" she asked.

"I can push it," said Joseph. "Then ride it home from the park." He could only walk her as far as the park, and then he had to turn back in case one of her parents might see. Up until the park, they could logically explain being in the same vicinity. Maman was probably busy throwing darts at the newspaper anyway.

"You don't have basketball practice?" asked Vonda.

"No," said Joseph. "Not today."

She shrugged, which meant "okay." Just once it would be nice if she looked really happy that he was around. Not like cheerleader-giddy or anything, but more than glad. Her smile filled him with happiness. He didn't enjoy feeling like a puppy following her around. Girls had ignored him until this year, but now he was catching some smiles and long looks. There wasn't a manual to help him know exactly what that meant, but it was nice that they were looking. His new dirt bike had come with an operating manual. It was much simpler to understand than smiles, stares, giggles, and shrugs.

Vonda chatted with him while he retrieved his bicycle. They joined the parade of students walking home from school. Joseph carefully took a position on the street side of the sidewalk. LaLa had said it was a gentlemanly thing to do. When he asked why, LaLa was a little vague. She said that when a man let a woman beside him walk next to the street, they were up to no good.

"Say, could you help me with a math problem when we get to the park?" asked Vonda. "It's just one."

"Sure," said Joseph. Vonda was in pre-algebra, so whatever the problem was, it was a piece of cake. Maybe Joseph could pretend to be perplexed and make it as big as two pieces. What a dilemma. Solve it quickly and maintain his smart status, or drag it out so he might brush his fingers across hers a few times as he worked it out on paper? As much as he wanted to slow-walk to lengthen their time together, it was all he could do not to jog to the park so that they could sit at the table side by side.

A kid who trailed them from the school kept gaining on them, but he wouldn't pass them on the sidewalk. Joseph turned and looked at him a few times. The kid sneered back like he was Doc Holliday in his long cowboy duster. All he was lacking was a Stetson hat. "You know him?" Joseph asked Vonda.

She looked over her shoulder. "It's a boy from my church," said Vonda. "I think he's always had a crush on me, but he's a real jerk. He's in the Posse Comitatus."

"Where'd they come up with a name like that?" asked Joseph. "It sounds like a body part in health class, like gluteus maximus."

"I think some of the men in our church are in the grown-up version of it," said Vonda. "Gluteus maximus fits them better. They're jerks, too."

Jerk. Shahla's worst insult to the male of the species. They must be bad.

The kid eventually turned off and went into a house. Joseph and Vonda continued to the park. The math problem was easy, and Joseph compromised. He showed her how easy it was, but he slowed the explanation to step-by-step instructions to stretch it out. He had her try one on her own to make sure she understood. The payoff was two brushes of their hands and several elbow touches.

Joseph's chest thumped uncontrollably when he was this close to her. Being alone with her made it worse. Even though he hadn't had practice, he was a little sweaty. *Please let the deodorant work.* Hair was growing under his arms, and although it didn't compare even remotely to Juan's, Joseph didn't understand how deodorant was supposed to work when there was a hairy barrier between the product and his skin. Reluctantly, Joseph said goodbye and watched Vonda walk toward the parsonage.

November was the start of basketball season. This time there'd been no fuss when Maman signed the release form. The sun set earlier now, and Joseph rode his bicycle home from the park. He was still sweaty, which made it chilly on the bike. He needed to cool off. Baba was home tonight, and he didn't want Baba to suspect he'd been in the park with Vonda. When he did something he wasn't supposed to do, it felt like the transgression was written all over his face. Glorious blue-eyed "Canon in D." Control. Smile. Smile. Smile.

No one was in the house, but the car was in the garage. Joseph put his bike away and searched. Maman and Baba weren't there. Maybe they'd gone for a walk. It was a good opportunity for Joseph to check on LaLa and see if she needed anything.

LaLa didn't need anything, but he found Maman and Baba. They were standing in LaLa's living room watching her television. Something bad must have happened. Silently, Joseph joined them. He absorbed the bigger story as images replayed. Americans who worked at the US Embassy were taken hostage at a university in Tehran. The Americans were blindfolded, marched through crazed, chanting crowds, and humiliated. The indignity welled into Joseph's chest. Who would dare treat Americans like this?

Iranians.

Oy veh. This was bad. Very bad.

Occasionally, Baba and Maman exchanged glances. Joseph saw their worry. Joseph had no real feelings for Iran, but for his parents, it had been home for the first thirty-plus years of their lives. Their families had lived there since King Nebuchadnez-zar conquered and captured the Jews of Jerusalem. Farsi was still the language and Iran still the land in their dreams. They had left Iran, but not because they wanted to. Joseph still didn't completely understand why.

They were in America, but their way of living in it was awkward. Maman still cooked Persian food. They spoke Farsi more than English. Joseph could see a warm, inner happiness when they joined with Iranian relatives for special events. They cooled to mere contentment here in this Texas town. The great courtesy of the Iranian people was so much a part of them. Now they stood befuddled watching the ultimate discourtesy playing out before them. Watching it replay in Miss Eleanor's home made it feel all the more awkward.

"Maybe the ayatollah will fix this," Baba muttered to himself. "This is not our Iran."

Bam! In spite of the serious scene replaying on the big console television, it hit Joseph. He'd always wondered why Baba allowed people to be rude to him, to dismiss him, to cut him off in midsentence. It was suddenly clear. Baba was a man of Middle Eastern hospitality. *Taarof*, humble courtesy, was more important than fast delivery of the information or agreement upon a deal. Their Dallas synagogue was mostly Jews of European descent, no different than any other white Americans. They didn't understand they were being discourteous to Baba.

Joseph had seen it on family visits to marketplaces in Israel. When a tourist asked the merchant how much a product cost, the tourist was only making a decision as to whether he wanted to buy it. To the merchant of Middle Eastern culture, however, the price negotiation had already begun. You didn't ask how much something cost unless you'd decided to buy it. That signaled the merchant to offer a cup of tea or sweets, even a chair, while the deal was hammered out. Joseph had witnessed the process many times, smirking when the American or European walked away without purchasing the item. It wasn't the way things were done. You didn't change your mind once you asked the price.

Americans didn't understand *taarof*, the complex Iranian social practice of extreme courtesies and humble politeness. When an Iranian said no, it may not really be no. It was a long, conversational dance that appeared fake to Americans, but it showed respect. When the synagogue *gabbai* offered Baba a refreshment, and Baba said no, the *gabbai* simply went to the next person. The *gabbai* was supposed to insist, to compliment, and Baba was supposed to give in with deep gratefulness.

Joseph had understood all along, or he wouldn't have known how discourteous it was. Only now, though, did he see that it wasn't intentional disrespect to Baba. They were simply speaking two different languages even though they both spoke English. The same went for how Baba interacted with cashiers or repairmen. Baba wasn't weak; he was respectful, but in an Iranian way.

Joseph looked at the television and back at his parents.

"I don' understand," said Maman. "I jus' don' understand. Firs' de Shah, and now dis."

"Trouble," whispered Baba.

29
NEIGHBOR HOOD

The Iran hostage crisis was a daily topic in Mrs. Draper's Texas history class. Suddenly, the explorations of the European nations to Texas and the trampling of Native American tribes were less interesting. Teachers and students talked about the hostages in Iran. Not that history had ever been interesting to Joseph. He liked to do things, not read about them. It would be more interesting to find some places that the Spanish explorers missed in Texas. Places with dirt, creeks, and mud. But not ticks.

The video of the bound and hooded hostages must have been running on a continuous loop on the evening news. It became harder for Joseph to hide his identity with Hispanic friends, nice clothes, good English grammar, and a team jersey. He worked harder to remove any accent. The discussion in current events class was peppered with explosive suggestions.

"Bomb them back into the Stone Age."

"Turn the Middle East into a sea of glass."

"Nuke 'em all."

Joseph had relatives in Iran, not just California. The letters from Iran stopped. Baba prayed earnestly for aunts, uncles, cousins, nephews, and nieces. When Maman prayed for them, tears streaked down her cheeks and she swayed from side to side, as if her body could move something in the universe.

Once when Joseph was too young to join his uncles on the men's side of the Wailing Wall in Jerusalem on an annual family holiday visit, he went with his mother to the women's side. He was probably four years old. There was an old woman who sat in a plastic chair clutching a tattered prayer book, face pressed hard against the ancient stones. She wore a faded, flowered headscarf. She wept uncontrollably while she prayed. Her face was a network of wrinkles as deep as the dry wadis of the Aravah desert.

The woman's sobs were gut-wrenching, and it scared Joseph. What could have happened to hurt this old grandmother? Other women tried to console her, offering plastic cups of water and tissues. They fanned her in the oppressive heat, but nothing interrupted the rivers of wet sorrow coming from so deep inside her. There was no one else in the world for the weeping woman but God.

Maman's prayers for her Iranian relatives were not that scary, but her tears of worry had a similar effect on Joseph. Like the ladies at the Wall, he wanted to do something, offer something, to console a pain so deep. It was a wound so nakedly awful that somehow only the One who made you deserved to see it.

The political situation was confused by the religious situation in Iran. Neither Baba nor Maman could explain it. Iranian history was complicated. Joseph wasn't allowed to spend a lot of time at LaLa's, so he couldn't watch TV for very long to find explanations. Would President Carter bomb Tehran and kill everyone? If he did, would the hostages be killed? Would the Jews in Iran be killed or arrested? Would they have all their property confiscated and be deported like Iraqi Jews? Joseph started pestering Baba for a television, but Baba said no. He didn't give a very convincing no, though, so Joseph kept trying.

The current events discussions at school made Joseph afraid and angry at the same time. Iran had nothing to do with why General Santa Anna marched to San Jacinto or that the Texas state bird was the mockingbird and the state flower was the bluebonnet. Mateo and Roberto kept his secret, but the other kids in their group knew he wasn't Hispanic. So did Larry. Would they snitch on him? Well, Joseph told Larry what he *wasn't*, not what he *was*, so maybe Larry wouldn't piece it together.

In the end, Joseph snitched himself out. It was a current events discussion in Mrs. Draper's Texas history class. Mrs. Draper halfheartedly rebuked a classmate for his suggestion to wipe out the entire Middle East. He said it in language that even Joseph wouldn't have used whether adults were present or not. In any other situation, the boy would have gone to the principal's office and suffered "licks" with the paddle board or three days in detention. It was too much.

Rage. Rage.

"Start here," said Joseph. The class grew quiet. Joseph liked talking in class, but he never participated in the current events discussion once the hostage crisis started. Baba had forbidden him from discussing anything about Iran.

"Right here," said Joseph, pointing to himself. "I was born in California, but my parents are from Iran. We're Jewish. We don't know what's happened to our relatives there. You want to bomb the whole country and kill everyone, including my family. I'll make it easy for you. Anybody want to go first?" He stood.

"Dude, sit down," Alex whispered behind him. "*Cállate.* Be cool."

There were several seconds of shocked silence before Mrs. Draper said, "Sit down, Joseph. No one wants to hurt you or your family."

"That's a lie," said Joseph.

And now here he sat in the principal's office. With justice like that, he should have called it a damn lie. In English. Because it was.

After ten minutes of waiting in the outer office, the principal, Mr. Lamb, opened his office door. He beckoned Joseph inside. Mrs. Draper sat there in those plastic, hoot-owl glasses. Mr. Lamb was one of the few men Joseph had ever seen who was taller than Baba. He was a gentle giant like Juan. His personality made students want to do what he said. You didn't want to disappoint Mr. Lamb, who always believed the best of the students. He seemed genuinely shocked when they broke the rules.

"Joseph, Mrs. Draper tells me you've been disrespectful to her."

"*I* was disrespectful to *her*?" asked Joseph.

Mrs. Draper sat there in her fashionable wedge haircut looking deeply wounded. Joseph decided he hated wedge haircuts. It looked like a chainsaw massacre near miss.

"You weren't?" asked Mr. Lamb, the dark shadows under his eyes deepening at the idea of this being anything more than a simple misunderstanding.

Mrs. Draper wasn't going to own up to any of this. Her word against Joseph's. There was only one way this was going to turn out. It wasn't like in a courtroom where Mr. Lamb would let him call a roomful of witnesses. Hostile witnesses at that.

"I don't believe I was," said Joseph, swallowing down what he wanted to say. Rage. Control.

"You didn't call her a liar?" asked Mr. Lamb.

"I said what she said was a lie. If that's disrespectful, then I said it," said Joseph.

"That's disrespectful," said Mr. Lamb.

Joseph clenched his teeth. Mr. Lamb wasn't going to ask if anyone had been disrespectful to him. "Could you put me in a different class?" said Joseph. There was another Texas history class this period. Mr. Chappelle probably didn't want to see him twice a day, but he doubted that Mr. Chappelle wasted extra time preparing a discussion on current events. He'd be in the teacher's lounge smoking and drinking coffee. Mr. Chappelle was a worksheet man through and through.

Mr. Lamb said, "First of all, you need to apologize to Mrs. Draper, don't you?"

It was maddening when adults forced you to say what they wanted when they knew you wouldn't mean it. Joseph wondered if Mrs. Draper would like to settle this with a game of dodgeball. He'd skin the rest of that wedge right off her head. Turn it into a bowl cut.

"Sorry."

Mr. Lamb nodded seriously. "Joseph, I don't think you need to change classes. Mrs. Draper feels as though it was just a simple misunderstanding. You're a good student," said Mr. Lamb. "And you have a chance at making it into the National Junior Honor Society this year."

"I don't want to be in her class," said Joseph.

"Then I'll need to call your parents," said Mr. Lamb. "If you and Mrs. Draper can work this out, we'll settle for an apology. If it's more serious than that, we need to have a parent conference."

A string of curse words in English, Farsi, Hebrew, Spanish, and Arabic ran through Joseph's head. No way. Baba was out of town. Maman would have no idea what was wrong or what to say. He'd have to translate for her. Baba would be angry with him for putting Maman in that position, for involving "the authorities."

"Look, Joseph, I'm sorry your family in Iran is experiencing difficulty in the political climate right now," said Mr. Lamb. "It has to be distressing to you and your family here, but you can't take it out on your teacher or the other students."

What had Mrs. Draper said to Mr. Lamb? Joseph slowly turned his head in a cold rage of disbelief to see if she'd look him in the eye. She merely gave him a fake look of sympathy.

Rage. Control. Rage. Control.

"I'll stay in class."

30
TOBOGGAN

Word about the Iranian family in town spread fast, maybe even before Joseph left basketball practice. When he rode his bike home, trash was in their front yard. Empty fast-food bags, drink cups, broken bottles. Joseph stopped to pick everything up before Maman saw it. He knew he was the cause of it. He could only blame the new blister in his gut on himself.

LaLa was in the kitchen. Maman had already seen the trash in the yard. She and LaLa were discussing what to do. LaLa wanted Maman and Joseph to come stay with her until Baba returned home. Maman was reluctant to do anything without asking Baba first. She didn't want to disturb him at work. She'd made a phone call to report the Shah of Iran's arrival, and she was afraid that calling his work again so soon would be frowned upon if it wasn't really an emergency.

In the end, Maman decided to stay at home, but LaLa reminded her of where the back-door key was to her house. LaLa assured her that the screen door wouldn't be latched in case she changed her mind. "Keep an eye on your mama," LaLa urged Joseph as she left. "And don't be afraid to call. If I need to get after someone with the garden rake, I will."

Joseph had no doubt that she would. After LaLa left, he drew the front window curtains. Dinner was filled with nervous small talk. They pretended it wasn't happening even though the trash may as well have been heaped on the kitchen table between them while they ate.

From time to time, Joseph peered out the front window after it grew dark. Some cars honked as they drove by that evening. The front yard collected empty cans, dirty towels, dirty diapers, and other trash thrown from passing traffic. Joseph was scared. What would he do without Baba? Baba was no fighter, but his size scared a lot of people. The best Joseph could do for protection was a baseball bat from when he tried to play Little League. Too many of the games were on Shabbat, so he gave up. The bat seemed so big when he was ten years old. Now it felt puny in his hands. He put the bat beside the front door.

Joseph brought his English homework to the front room so he could keep his ears open in case someone came closer than the street. He couldn't concentrate. For the life of him, he couldn't find the participles and gerunds in the sentences.

Maman made her get-ready-for-bed noises. The refrigerator door opened and closed, so she'd put his lunch sack for the next day in there. That would be peanut butter and jelly. No Eye-rainian entrees to scare Vonda, please. A quarter and a dime clacked onto the kitchen table. Milk money. A soft click. The kitchen light turned out. Steps creaked on the wooden hallway floor all the way to her bedroom. "Go to bed soon, Youssef-jun," she called.

"*Baleh*, Maman," Joseph called back. He went back to the hunt for the elusive words on the worksheet. His English average was hovering at a high B. He wanted to tip the scale to an A so Baba wouldn't give him a hard time about football next year. He could be inducted into the National Junior Honor Society for the spring term. First, he had to find some dangling participles. Something that was dangling should be a lot easier to find. Maybe he could call Mateo to find out what exactly he was looking for. Joseph looked up at the clock on the mantel over the fireplace. It was already 10:00 p.m. That was too late to be calling about homework.

When he looked back to the worksheet, headlights turning into the driveway lit up the living room through the curtains. Joseph looked up and waited to see if it was just a turnaround. The lights pulled in closer, all the way up to the house. Gingerly, Joseph set the worksheet on the coffee table. He listened. The door to Maman's bathroom closed, and he heard the water running.

The vehicle remained, and Joseph could hear the engine. It was a truck, which matched the height of the headlights. Then the headlights went dark. Nothing happened for several minutes. Joseph debated whether to take Maman through the back door and sneak her across to LaLa, who could drive them to Dallas. Should he call the police first? Joseph's fear turned into anger. Why would Baba leave them alone when he knew these people were hateful?

Joseph went to the window and pulled back the curtain slightly. The cab light came on in the truck, and a dark figure emerged. Then the man stopped. He reached inside and took something from a gun rack mounted on the back window of the truck. It briefly flashed under the security light on the electrical pole. Joseph saw the barrel of a long gun. Oh, no. *Please, God, how do I protect Maman?* Joseph raced to the door of his parents' bathroom. He rapped on the door loudly. "Maman! Get dressed. Hurry!"

Joseph sprinted back to the living room. He parted the curtains to check the progress of the boo in the driveway. It was too late. He heard light footsteps on the wooden front steps. The shadow crossed the wooden porch boards to the other window. The man was wearing a toboggan. Maybe he wasn't so tall. But he carried a shotgun.

From down the hall, the sound of Maman's footsteps moved toward him. She was out of the shower, and she'd thrown on her clothes. The look on her face was anything but scared, though. She gripped the poker from the fireplace they rarely used. Good grief. That wasn't very Maman-like, but it wouldn't do much good against a shotgun. Maman didn't bother with English, and her long hair was down. It was black, damp, and wild. "Did one of those sons of bitches come to our door?"

As grave as the situation was right outside the window, in disbelief, Joseph looked her in the eyes. Well, he didn't have to worry about Maman hearing him call someone a *pedar sagg* anymore. She stood there like an angry mama bear. Joseph held up a hand so she wouldn't bust through the front door hunting a shooter with a poker.

Joseph picked up the baseball bat and tiptoed quickly to the other front window. He pulled the curtain back slightly and peered through. If the man did come through the front door, it would take extra seconds for him to kick or shoot through the lock. That would give them a few seconds to run out the back door to LaLa's.

The man in the toboggan stood on the porch, his back to the front door. He looked out at the street. The knot in Joseph's stomach got tighter. What if the man was a decoy? What if the real shooter was coming through the back door at that very moment? Would they run straight into another gun if they ran out the back to LaLa's house?

After he'd taken a long, 180-degree look at the neighborhood, the man sat on the porch swing. He rested the gun across his knees. In the porchlight, Joseph could see who it was, and relief flooded over him. It was Mr. Ybarra. He set a large thermos on the porch deck before he leaned back in the swing.

"It's just Mr. Ybarra, Maman," said Joseph, trying to be nonchalant. "Looks like he's keeping an eye on the place."

Maman went to the window and pulled back the curtain. After she was satisfied that there was no danger, she dropped the curtain. She took a long look at Joseph's baseball bat. He took an equally long look at the poker. Although Joseph's emotions right then were doing crazy things to his heart and gut, he laughed. Maman laughed. She hugged him close. "My little lion," she said softly. "This is what life was like for us at times in Iran. I'm not so scared as you think I am. There was peace for Jews, then not so much peace. We had kind neighbors there, too. This will pass, or we'll go to Dallas. Don't worry."

Joseph dreaded going to school the next day, but he was less worried about leaving Maman alone than he would have been before she barreled down the hallway with the fireplace poker. He'd have never guessed that Maman was more afraid of making a wrong turn on the interstate than of a redneck making a wrong turn into her house. Now Joseph had a first of all firsts to report to Shahla next Sunday. Maman had used a curse word.

As he pedaled his bike to school, Joseph's mood swung between dread and a grin at Maman's "*pedar sagg.*"

At school, Joseph stopped Mateo in the hallway before homeroom. "Your papá came to our house last night," said Joseph. "I got up this morning to pick up the trash in our yard before Maman saw it, and he was gone. He'd already picked up the trash."

"Yeah," said Mateo. "There was some bad talk going around town after your little outburst in Mrs. Draper's class. Papi asked me if your baba was home, and I told him that he was out of town working. Papi talked to lots of our family and friends, and the men are going to take turns spending the night until your baba comes home. They think it will die down in a few weeks. Papi says the worst actors in town are all talk, and there's not many of them. They just like to stir things up down at the honky-tonk at night when they get drunk. Makes a bunch of losers feel patriotic or something. Papi's going to talk to your baba about calling the police. Maybe they can drive by your house more often."

"Baba will never call the police," said Joseph. "He's afraid of them."

Mateo shrugged. "Folks like us stick together. It's not always easy to get police to help when you speak Spanish. They throw everybody in jail and let the judge sort it out later. My older brother Eddie just got accepted to the law school at University of Texas. He wants to be a judge."

It would be nice if more Hispanics were policemen. That way people wouldn't be thrown in jail for speaking Spanish in the first place, but being a judge sounded cool, too. "Well, tell your papá thank you for me," said Joseph. "But it's awful cold for them to sit on the porch all night."

"Papi grew up on a ranch," said Mateo. "You can't kill him with cold or heat, that's for sure."

Men in dark toboggans and thick coats came each night after sundown. They remained on the porch until just before sunrise. It was improper for Maman to speak to them, but she fixed them pots of hot tea. She sent Joseph out before bedtime with reheated supper servings and sweets. Joseph wasn't sure what the men thought about rolled grape leaf *dolmeh, adas polo* rice, and *ash'e gureh* soup, but they cleaned up every bite. Every spoonful.

───────

When Baba came home the next Friday evening, Joseph met him at the door. "Maybe we should talk outside first?" Joseph suggested.

Baba frowned at Joseph's seriousness. He put down his bag, hard hat, and briefcase. They sat on the porch swing, and Joseph told him everything. At first, Baba didn't say anything. He stared across the porch as if seeing something seven thousand miles away. And maybe he was.

"Youssef, you will go with your mother when she goes to the market. Anywhere. You will not allow her to go anywhere alone when I am not home. Understood?"

"*Baleh*, Baba." But how did Baba expect Joseph not to "allow" Maman to do anything? She was the grown-up. The danger of angry neighbors was very real, but Baba's wording was strange. His father was always very protective of Maman. Joseph knew it was their culture. In some ways, Baba treated her like a child, but always with dignity. Like she was a little princess tragically banished to a strange land called Texas. It wasn't really a Jewish thing. The other men at the synagogue didn't act the same as Baba and other Persian men. Roberto called it *macho*. Joseph thought *macho* meant being very masculine, but there was more to it.

"If Maman needs to go somewhere, and you're not here, then she will ask Miss Eleanor for help. It's important that you both stay out of sight as much as possible so that the neighbors are not provoked," said Baba.

How could seeing a kid and his mom provoke anyone?

"If matters don't improve here, then I'll send you both to Be'er Sheva to stay with her relatives in Israel. You are old enough to be enrolled in a yeshiva or public school there. Your Hebrew is good enough. Things won't be better in Dallas as long as the Americans are hostage."

What? Oh, no. He'd made the basketball team, and he was good. The pickup games at the park were great preparation. The coaches said all Joseph needed was some sharpening, and he could start playing the center position. His muscles were filling out, so he'd be even better at football next year. His new dirt bike. Flying lessons on Sundays. How could he leave Vonda? Joseph's secret dream was to fly fighter jets, not to sit in a religious school and study all day.

"When things calm down here, I can send for you."

How long would that be? How would he get letters to Vonda? Would she forget him and be attracted to another boy? Maybe a white one who hated Iranians?

Baba sighed. "If you and Maman need to live in Israel, I'll visit as often as I can. I never thought the danger here would be worse than the danger there. At least there, you have relatives to look after you."

No. Please, no. Baba was gone so much already. Shabbat was their island of peace. It was Baba's job to keep them safe here, not to ship them off for Maman's crazy brothers to babysit. Summer visits to Israel were nice, but Joseph always missed Baba, especially on Shabbat evening when his cousins huddled around their fathers for blessings. How could you ever make up for missing Shabbat blessings? It's not like you could pile them on later.

Every good thing was slipping from his grasp.

31

HANDY CAP

Joseph thought Vonda would be a haven in his storm. Instead, she suggested that they eat with their own friends until things blew over. The look on his face must have made her feel bad, because she offered to exchange daily notes.

"Notes?" asked Joseph. He was horrible at writing. His participles and gerunds ran untamed across the worksheets. Mrs. Thornton didn't appreciate his joke about pronouns being professional nouns, so his English grade was still dangling between an A and a B.

"Yeah," said Vonda. "You're the talk of the school right now. If people talk about you, then they may talk about us. If my dad heard about it . . ."

Funny she hadn't worried about it before, but it did make sense. Her family was much more in the town gossip loop than Baba. He barely knew anyone but the Ybarras, Miss Eleanor, and a few men who also worked for the oil company. "Notes?" asked Joseph again. Girls wrote notes. Not boys. Joseph needed someone to talk to other than Roberto, who dismissed all the bomb-Iran craziness with his usual, "Dumbasses." Joseph needed a blue-eyed "Canon in D" duet.

"Yeah. I already write you notes sometimes. Let's write a note back and forth and exchange it each day. It could be fun," said Vonda.

"Can I still walk you to class?"

"Well . . ."

Well? She wasn't sure? The hated tears threatened to well up, but Joseph fought them back. He wasn't allowed to be angry, either, and being angry made him teary. He had to not feel anything. Rage. Control. Smile. Fly above it.

"Never mind," said Joseph.

"So you're not mad?" she asked.

When did it ever matter whether Joseph was mad? He said, "I'm not angry. Mad people are crazy people. I'm not crazy."

Vonda smiled and handed him a folded sheet of notebook paper. "I'm glad."

That was the start of their correspondence and the end of their conversations.

Joseph was no good at writing. What did a girl like Vonda want to talk about? Their lunchroom conversations were easy back-and-forth. A note required at least twenty-four hours for a response. The first line told him she'd decided on the separation long before she suggested it.

I'm sorry, Joseph. I'm going to miss having lunch with you. You're really funny and smart. I wish I could do math like you.

Yeah, me to.

Are you mad at me?

I think we already covered that. No. Not angry. Just dissappointed. I miss you.

I miss you, too. I always expect to look up and see you when I'm at Miss Eleanor's for lessons. You're really good at playing the piano. Will you be at the recital?

I don't spend as much time at Miss Eleanor's anymore. I can't play in the recitals because they are on Shabbat. Did you know that you can play all Emily Dickinson's poems to the tune of "Yellow Rose of Texas"?

That is SOOOOO funny, Joseph. I tried it, and you're right. Mrs. Thornton would have a heart attack.

Do you like poetry?

Yes, I really like poetry. It's more interesting than the short stories in English class. I write poetry in my diary. I'm too embarrassed for anyone to read it.

I wouldn't laugh if you let me read one of your poems. My parents read a lot of Persian poetry, but they read it in Farsi. Not Farisi.

You always make me laugh. It's Pharisee, not Farisi. Can you translate any of it into English?

Your wish is my command. It's not like English poetry, though. It doesn't rhyme in English . . . "Ever since Happiness heard your name, it runs through the streets trying to find you." The Persian poet Hafiz wrote that. He lived a long time ago. You won't let me read one of your poems?

That's very romantic. I think that's "personification." Or maybe "metaphor." Mrs. Thornton would be proud.

Hafiz wrote it, not me. Can I walk you home as far as the park on Friday? I don't have practice. No one can say anything if we both have to go home that way.

That may not be a good idea. Translate some more poetry for me.

Okay, here you go. 1. "Your heart and my heart are very, very old friends." 2. "The subject tonight is love. And the subject for tomorrow night, to. As a matter of fact, there is no better topic for us to discuss until we all die." Hafiz wrote those. He's a very romantic poet. Kind of like Pachelbel's "Canon in D." It takes two to enjoy him.

Middle Eastern men must be very romantic. You're the only person I know from the Middle East. Joseph is in the Bible, but it seems like a strange name for someone from the Middle East.

I was born in Los Angeles, not the Middle East. My real name is Youssef. I always go by the teachers' desk on the first day of class and ask if they will pencil in Joseph. Saves me a lot of greif when they call roll the first time. It's only translated Joseph in English Bibles. The Bible was written in Hebrew, so it's really pronounced Yosef, like mine in Farsi. Could we talk for a minute on Wednesday before I go to gym class?

Okay. Come to my locker.

Thanks for talking to me. Did you like the card?

It was very nice. I put it in my diary with your other notes.

Wow. I made the diary? Maybe one day you'll send me a poem. Heres another one. "The Heart is a thousand-stringed instrument that can only be tuned with Love." Bigger than a piano, huh?

Yes, that's a pretty big instrument. By the way, are things getting better for you?

Not really. We still get trash in the yard.
Someone wrote something really bad on my
locker, but the janiter allready got most of
it off before I saw it.

I'm sorry that's happening to you. I read about the Persian
Jews in the Book of Esther in Sunday school class. You have an
interesting heritage. Our family is from Germany. I mean, not like
Nazi or anything. Our family was here before World War 2.

I guess that's where you get such pretty blue
eyes. When do you think we can meet and talk? I
really miss you.

Dad and Mom go to a ministers' retreat each winter. One of my
older sisters will come home from college to stay with me for
the weekend. I could slip out for a while and she wouldn't say
anything.

When????

32
HAT SHOP

Maman sniffed grapes. She sniffed tomatoes. She sniffed melons. Joseph dreaded trips to the grocery store. He stood by with the cart, rolling the wheels back and forth while she inspected every potential fruit or vegetable. It was maddening. She held the fruit, sniffed it, tested its texture. She turned it around and around checking for over-ripeness or bad spots. She held her ear close and thumped. She carefully weighed it. She returned some to the bin or added more. She squinted at the numbers on the scale. When they finally made it through the produce section, she knew to the penny and pound how much she'd purchased.

If the cashier tossed her careful selections onto the scale, Maman's expression turned to a frown. Today was one of those days. The Piggly Wiggly cashier flung the apples onto the scale. The apples bounced and skittered inside the bag. "Tell her not to bruise the fruit," Maman told Joseph in Farsi.

"It's okay, Maman," Joseph said. Baba said they were to keep a low profile as long as the Americans were held hostage.

It wouldn't be smart to cause a disturbance over a dent in an apple. This wasn't friendly territory. Maman's headscarf sometimes caused a stir in the aisles or checkout line when people realized that she wasn't wearing it to conceal hair curlers or chemo treatments. The scarf screamed that the woman wearing it didn't belong in a grocery store named after a pig.

"No, she's ruining my fruit," insisted Maman, still in Farsi. "Tell her to be careful. I won't pay for what she ruins."

The cashier glanced up, sensing Maman's objection was related to something she was doing.

"Please, Maman," said Joseph. "She's not hurting the fruit."

"Yes, she did," said Maman. "She bruised that apple."

"I'll eat it in the car," said Joseph. "It won't have time to rot."

"This is unacceptable," said Maman, pleading her case to Joseph for translation into English. She thrust her hands forward, palms upward. It was a Middle Eastern gesture that really didn't translate into English. She wanted Joseph to make her case for undamaged fruit.

Joseph didn't know why he did it, but he did. He lifted his chin back at Maman, a gesture that his baba sometimes used. It meant the argument was over. Joseph instantly felt guilty. It was too late, though. The store manager was correcting something on the cash register in the checkout line next to them. He stepped over with a clipboard, bifocals slid down his nose. "Is there a problem here?" he asked.

Maman wasn't confident speaking English, but she understood a lot. She extended her fingers toward the evidence, two apples that had rolled out of the plastic bag down to the bagging area.

"Do you speak English, ma'am?" the manager practically yelled.

Good grief. She wasn't deaf. Now they had the attention of everyone in the front of the store.

"I speak English," said Joseph as quietly as he could.

"De apples," said Maman. "I don' pay for de hurting apples. Two hurting apples is forty-four cent."

"Hurting apples?" asked the manager, managing to arch his eyebrows upward while his mouth and bushy mustache arched downward. The manager had extraordinary facial hair control.

"Yes, she trow de apples down," said Maman, but this wasn't the Middle East. There, merchants specialized in meat, dairy, fruits, or vegetables. They prided themselves on the quality of their selection. In the open-air markets or sidewalk stands, merchants sliced open deep-ruby pomegranates and bright-pink melons to entice customers to taste their sweetness and smell their freshness. They hovered over their customers like a mother following a toddler. They selected the best fruits for the customer. They assured with every breath that this was the freshest, sweetest, or crispest in the entire city. In the Middle East, you don't trow de apples or anything else.

"It's okay," said Joseph to the manager. "I think the lady just dropped them."

"Where are y'all from?" asked the manager.

"Seventh Street," said Joseph. "Really, it's not a problem."

The manager paused suspiciously. Maman interrupted, "Yes, is problem. I don' wan' to pay for dem."

"Wait, aren't y'all those Iranians?" said the manager.

Eye-rainians. Well, great. Here we go. "It doesn't matter," said Joseph. "I'll put those two apples back."

"I already rang 'em up," said the cashier to the manager as if the man hadn't just deleted a charge off the cash register next to them.

The cash register rhythm of the checkout lines on either side faded to an uneasy standstill, like when the school band started wrong in marching practice. Maman and Joseph had stopped everything, two trumpets playing the wrong song. The customers and cashiers looked at Maman as if she'd been uncorked from a genie bottle. Not a blonde-haired, blue-eyed, sexy *I Dream of Jeannie*, but a dark-skinned, raghead nightmare genie from Eye-ran.

"I was born in California," said Joseph. "Not Iran."

"Well, you can just tell your mama to do her grocery shopping in California . . . or Iran. Wherever she's from," said the manager in a drawl. "Ain't much difference." A few nods of the head in the checkout lines affirmed the manager's banishment decree from their happy, hometown Piggly kingdom.

Maman had given up on the conversation between Joseph and the manager. She'd gone around to collect the two hurting apples from the bagging area. Rage. Control. As badly as Joseph wanted to lob the entire bag of apples at the manager, cashier, and everyone standing there, he took the two bruised apples from Maman's hand. He put them back on the counter. Gently.

"What . . . ?" she asked, but Joseph shook his head.

"Come on, we're going, Maman," said Joseph in Farsi.

"But why?" she protested. Maman already knew how much the groceries would cost, to the penny. She pulled the cash and change from her dress pocket. Then she started to pluck forty-four cents in coins from the total. Joseph shook his head again and folded his hand over hers.

"Put it away, Maman, we're leaving," said Joseph. He took her by the elbow and guided her out the automatic doors. Behind them, Joseph could hear murmurs of indignation.

Iranians!

Of all the nerve . . .

Did you see how she was dressed?

Could you even understand what she said?

Just marched in here and started harassing the cashier like they owned the place . . .

Maman finally realized that it wasn't a simple fruit misunderstanding. "I don't understand, Youssef," said Maman when she started the car.

No. She wouldn't.

"They know we are Iranian, Maman. Let's go to Rehkopf's."

"They don't have good fruits and vegetables," she objected.

"Then Safeway," said Joseph.

"But it's farther from home . . ."

"Let it go, Maman. Just let it go."

33
BLACK HATS

If Joseph wasn't so curious about what Baba had to say about the Piggly Wiggly, it would have been one more case where Joseph felt Baba was a coward. Baba listened to Joseph's description of what happened. He nodded his head. "I'm proud of you, Youssef," he said. "You did exactly the right thing."

It would be nice if Joseph felt the same. About both things.

"Why did we move here, Baba?" asked Joseph. "We could live in Dallas."

"It would be easier," said Baba. "But what happened at the grocery store is exactly what I'd expect in a town this size. People who aren't from the neighborhood stand out."

That was mad crazy. "You moved here because you *wanted* us to stand out?" asked Joseph.

"No, so others would stand out," said Baba. "If anyone from Iran tried to find us and meant us harm, then it would be much harder for them not to be noticed. This was a good location. Close to the office, close to the synagogue in Dallas, close to one of my company's airfields."

"Who's looking for us?" asked Joseph.

"No one I know of," said Baba, and that was the end of the conversation. A tiny television did appear in Baba's study, though, "strictly for news." With some negotiation, Sunday football was added to the authorized list. Was there ever anything Joseph would be able to decide on his own?

School didn't get any better. In the hallway, things were miserable. Joseph kept finding trash and nasty notes slipped into his locker between classes.

Sand nigger.

Raghead.

Dune coon.

Camel jockey.

Towelhead.

Joseph was sometimes jostled in the crowded hallway or poked hard. When he turned around, he saw only blank or grinning faces in the swarm. Shouted insults hung above the racket of class changes.

At first, Joseph raked the trash from his locker into the hallway. That got him a lecture from Mr. Chappelle about dropping trash around his locker. He had to miss the first fifteen minutes of basketball practice because he agreed to come back and clean the whole eighth-grade hallway after school. That was better than forty-five minutes of detention. Coach made him run laps to make up the fifteen minutes. The next day, Joseph brought a plastic bag to hang from the coat hook of his locker. He collected the trash to throw away later.

Joseph wanted to fight, but if he did, Baba would surely

whip him again, probably send him to Israel to religious school. Between sixth and seventh period one day, Joseph put away his English book in his locker. He pulled out his gym bag. He thought for a moment about homework. All he had was math, and he'd finished it in class. Just as Joseph shut the locker door and twirled the combination lock, someone kicked his gym bag hard. The blow hit the bag against the side of his leg, and it knocked him off balance.

Joseph dropped the bag and whirled, determined not to let his attacker slip away in the crowd again. This time, his attackers were many. They weren't sneaking off. Unfortunately, Mr. Chappelle wasn't there to monitor the trash around his locker. Five boys from the Posse Comitatus formed a horseshoe around him. The other students milled behind them uneasily, sensing a fight. Joseph still had no idea what Posse Comitatus meant. Apparently, it was an anti-Joseph-Nissan-the-Iranian-dune-coon organization.

"Go home, towelhead," said the biggest one. Joseph thought the biggest one was the leader of the group. None of them wore their long dusters or cowboy hats today. Big clue.

"I am home," said Joseph. "And you go to hell." He looked around. "All of you."

They didn't go to hell. Three of them went for him at once. Two lagged, maybe not as committed as the other three. Joseph ducked a punch and hit the biggest guy first. Someone punched Joseph above the kidney, which took his breath away. It felt like stepping off into the deep end of a swimming pool. Another boy swung on Joseph with a sock. Inside was a locker combination padlock, and Joseph's face exploded with hot pain. The biggest boy recovered. He threw a hard punch into Joseph's left cheek. Another boy grabbed for him.

Joseph knew he couldn't stay up, so he drove his legs as if he were tackling. He grabbed the biggest boy's hips, drilling him down to the hallway floor and collapsing atop him. Hands grabbed at him to pull him off, but Joseph kneed the boy square in the groin with everything he had. The Boss of the Posse writhed sideways and grabbed himself. Now the others started kicking Joseph. He desperately tried to crawl to the lockers so he could use them to defend his backside. His right eye was already swelling shut. Out of sheer fear and determination, Joseph made it back to his feet.

This was way worse than the tussle with the Edmondsons. Joseph knew he was going to lose this one. Badly. The sock flew again. Joseph threw up an arm, but it was hard to see. After that, Joseph only knew he was on the floor again. He lost track of blows. The rest of the Posse took turns kicking him. One blow that smashed into his left side was agonizing.

Suddenly, the blows stopped. Joseph heard Larry Edmondson's voice. Great. All he needed was for Larry and Brian to finish him off for the Posse. Instead, not another kick landed. The semicircle of sneakers and boots around him shuffled, widened, and moved back. Larry used the most admirable combination of curse words, and Joseph looked up. Lock Boy was on the floor. Larry held the lock in the sock, brandishing it at the crowd. "Come on," Larry threatened. "And if you're too chicken, then stick your tails between your sorry asses and get outta here. He ain't done nothin' to you."

Roberto pushed through the crowd and wedged himself between Joseph and the closest Posse boys. Joseph struggled to get up, and Roberto helped him to stand and lean against the lockers. It really wasn't clear to Joseph whether all his parts were working. The cool lockers were a welcome prop.

"Go on," said Larry. "You ain't no posse; you're a bunch of . . ." He inserted a curse word that Joseph had never even dared to try.

The rest of the Posse helped Lock Boy and the Boss get to their feet. Roberto postured up, which moved some Hispanic faces into the semicircle. The Posse was now outnumbered. Larry twirled the sock around his hand tightly and punched the Boss hard. Lock Boy turned to leave. Larry kicked him in the rear end to motivate him.

One of the other booted Posse members backed away. He smirked at Larry. "You ain't nothing but white trash, Edmondson. Everybody knows your daddy ain't nothing but a jailbird and your momma ain't nothing but a truck-stop slut. This ain't over." Juan Garza's big black head of hair bobbed into view above the crowd. That was all it took for it to indeed be over. The warning bell rang, which meant they had sixty seconds to make it to the gym for seventh period.

"You okay, kid?" asked Larry.

"Yeah," said Joseph. But he wasn't.

"Dude, you look like hell," said Roberto.

Joseph was too weary and sore to say something sarcastic. Instead, he said, "I guess I made us tardy to seventh period. Coach will have us running laps around the gym until 5:30 tonight."

"I don't think you could run a lap around your kitchen table right now," said Roberto.

Larry picked up Joseph's gym bag, Roberto took Joseph by the arm, and Juan walked on the other side of him. The few students left in the hallway scampered to class. Joseph was glad that Juan was there. Roberto would be late to study hall, but the study hall teacher always let him go to the shop class and help the teacher clean up. He wouldn't be missed.

Joseph walked slowly, bent so that he could breathe without feeling like a knife was stuck in his ribs. The basketball coach was calling roll when they walked in. The locker room was quiet. All the students already knew. After one look at him, the coach knew, too. "Go to my office and wait, Nissan," was all he said. He went back to calling roll. Roberto whispered, "Later," and he left Joseph with Juan and Larry.

Juan went to his place on the bench for roll call. Larry set down Joseph's gym bag at the door of the office and turned to go to his bench. A weird feeling of loneliness washed over Joseph, and he said, "Hey, Larry . . ."

Larry turned.

"Could you . . . maybe . . . come into the office with me?"

Joseph didn't know why he said it. It felt like he was about to step over a cliff. He wanted to cry. Normally, he could talk himself out of it, but he had nothing left right now, physically or mentally. His logical mind had gone into hiding. No rage. No control. He was empty and scared even though the fight was over.

Larry tossed his head slightly to move the long hair out of his eyes. There was the cat. But there was no taunting this time. "Yeah, kid," said Larry. "Come on."

34

WHITE HATS

Larry pushed open the office door, and Joseph shuffled in. Other coaches were in the gym office, and they stared. It was Coach Meeks who broke the silence. "Nissan, what the *hell* have you got into?"

Joseph shrugged. "I fell down."

Coach Meeks looked at Larry. "What happened, Edmondson?"

Larry moved to Joseph's side. "He fell down."

There was a long silence. Coach Meeks looked back and forth between them. When neither Larry nor Joseph added anything, Coach dismissed Larry. "Go dress out, Edmondson."

Larry had a deep voice, but he asked Joseph softly, "You gonna be okay?"

"Yeah," said Joseph. "Thanks."

There was no basketball practice for Joseph the rest of the week. There was detention.

It was a mess. A blur. The nurse examined him. She said he needed to go to the emergency room for X-rays on his cheekbone and ribs. Mr. Lamb called Baba to the school. Baba had to promise to accompany Joseph to Mr. Lamb's office the next morning with a doctor's report. Joseph had no broken ribs, but the doctor wrote a note that said he had severe bruising and a possible concussion. He had to sit out of sports for at least a week and be watched for symptoms from the blow to his head.

Normally, Joseph would want to tell Baba what happened. Not now. The Shabbat incident with the Edmondsons at Rehkopf's store didn't leave him much hope that there were any excuses. And he just hurt. Inside and out. He didn't want to talk about it. He wanted to forget it.

"Sorry, Baba," was all he said when Baba arrived to take him to the hospital. And it was all he would say. Baba let him be quiet. When they got home, Joseph took a shower, made his prayers, and went to bed without supper. He added a prayer of thanks that Baba was there to pick him up instead of Maman. The look on her face when she'd seen him had melted him inside. He couldn't imagine her having to deal with the school staff and hospital staff alone.

The next morning, the main office was full of the Posse Comitatus and their parents. Joseph, Baba, and Larry Edmondson were shepherded into an assistant principal's office. Larry didn't say where his parents were, but the assistant principal already knew they wouldn't be coming. Back and forth Mr. Lamb and the assistant principal went, gathering information. Joseph heard Roberto and Juan paged to Mr. Lamb's office over the intercom along with some other students. Maybe it was those who saw what happened. No matter who asked, Joseph didn't answer any questions.

Just before lunchtime, the assistant principal walked Joseph and Baba over to Mr. Lamb's office. The Posse was gone. Mr. Lamb motioned to the chairs so they would have a seat.

"Joseph," said Mr. Lamb. "I'm sorry this has happened to you."

Joseph stared at Mr. Lamb's desk nameplate. It was hand-made from a block of wood, likely from someone in shop class. Roberto could make a better one than that. He made stall name-plates for all the horses in Mr. Ybarra's barn: Sonora. Yellow Jacket. Dash. Corona. Doc. Easy Babe. Go-Go Girl. Santana.

"Joseph!"

Joseph blinked. Mr. Lamb's eyebrows were raised. Baba put a big hand over Joseph's forearm. "Are you okay?" he asked.

"*Baleh*, Baba," said Joseph. His thoughts had wandered dreamily. Maybe that's what a concussion was. Easy Babe. He liked that name. Easy. He'd told Fereshteh that he had a girl-friend, but he really didn't. Not that easy.

Mr. Lamb said, "Joseph, you've been having a tough time. Your friends tell me that you've been getting nasty notes and trash in your locker. I wish you'd come and talked to me. There were some things I could do."

"We already talked. There's nothing you can do," said Joseph. "There's nothing anyone can do." He didn't care if it sounded cheeky. What did he have to lose? He was probably going to be on the next flight to Tel Aviv. His mind drifted to Mr. Ybarra's barn and the smell of sweet hay. Easy Babe.

"We never know until we try, Joseph," said Mr. Lamb. "And I really need to hear from you exactly what happened yesterday. It can make the difference between whether I treat this as a fight or an assault. Everything points toward an assault. I'll call the police if you'll tell me what happened."

"No police," said Joseph before Baba could. "It was my fault. I cursed at them. I shouldn't have cursed." There was no way he would make Baba face the police.

"Maybe you cursed at them," said Mr. Lamb, "but this was a planned attack. Those five boys knew there was no teacher on duty in the eighth-grade hallway between sixth and seventh period because Mr. Chappelle was covering study hall yesterday. They also knew that your friends wouldn't be close at that class change. I know all five of them either hit or kicked you. Please, son, tell me what happened. You have to help me to help you."

"No, sir." The less talking, the sooner they'd leave him alone.

Mr. Lamb sighed and looked at Baba. Baba shook his head. "He won't tell me, either," said Baba.

Mr. Lamb said, "The boys have been warned against having this kind of gang at the school. We're going to talk to all the parents of the boys who have been identified with Posse Comitatus, not just the ones who jumped you. Since the fight was so lopsided, I have the option of putting you in after-school detention for a week instead of suspending you with the other boys. If you won't talk, then I'll have to put you in detention hall. Your friends and some of the other students have tried to help you, but no one really saw how it started."

"Detention is fine," said Joseph. If he even made it there before he made it to the airport.

"Help me understand your rule," said Baba. "Five boys attack my son, and he is punished?"

"Yes, Mr. Nissan," said Mr. Lamb. "That is school policy for a fight. No matter who started it, everyone must be punished. It is only in the type of punishment that I have flexibility. Joseph and Larry will have to go to five days of detention hall."

"It's okay, Baba," said Joseph. "The doctor said I couldn't go to basketball practice anyway. I don't mind spending it in detention."

Baba said to Mr. Lamb, "I could have stayed in Iran for such a policy." He stood and tapped Joseph on the shoulder. "Come, Youssef." Joseph stood. "Look at my son," said Baba. He paused, and Mr. Lamb did focus his big, sad eyes on Joseph's disfigured face. "What will I say to his mother?"

"I'm sorry, Mr. Nissan," said Mr. Lamb. "I really, really am. Please let me turn this over to the local police."

"Youssef?" asked Baba.

"No, sir."

———————

After school that day, Mr. Delafield checked off Joseph's name on the detention roster. Joseph took a seat in the back near Larry. The other students were looking at him. He was tired of being looked at. His face was an ugly, swollen wreck. He'd been nauseated all day. After three separate sessions of staring into a toilet for most of between-class time, he couldn't throw up. Joseph pulled out his books from the morning classes he'd missed. A minute later, a commotion at the front of the room made Joseph look up.

Mateo was standing at the teacher's desk. Mateo? In detention? Never.

"Your name's not on the roster, Mateo," said Mr. Delafield, who looked equally as puzzled.

"Then you can write it in," said Mateo. "I'm staying."

"What in the world for?" asked Mr. Delafield. The other

students looked around at each other. Too Many Tardies. Talking in Class. Chewing Gum in Class. Bad Language. Writing on the Desk. Smoking in the Bathroom. Fighting.

"For nothing," said Mateo.

"What?" said Mr. Delafield. "Go on, now, Mateo. You're disrupting."

"My friend is in detention hall for nothing, so I want to sit in detention hall for nothing, too," said Mateo. Roberto walked in with a couple of books under his arm. And Juan. And a few boys from the basketball team. And some kids that Joseph had helped in math class. And some of the football team. A couple of the girls from Vonda's clique. Nearly twenty students pushed into the room and surrounded the desk, causing Mr. Delafield to stand up in a panic.

"No, Mateo, get these students out of here . . ."

"Everyone in the school knows what happened," said Mateo. "We can't change school policy, but we can sit in detention with them."

"No, no you can't," said Mr. Delafield.

Larry watched. A twitch of amusement showed around his cat eyes. Otherwise, he remained as aloof as Joseph.

"Why not?" asked Mateo. "Is it somewhere in school policy that a student can't go to detention hall? Because if so, I missed it." Mateo added, "Because I looked."

Of course he did.

"I . . . I don't know." Mr. Delafield's easy extra-duty money was getting uneasy. Easy Babe.

Smokers, Gum Chewers, Tardies, and other offenders smirked, but Mateo was dead serious.

"Uh . . . I'll tell you what," said Mr. Delafield. "I'll check with Mr. Lamb in the morning, and if you want to come to detention hall tomorrow, he can decide if it's okay."

Mateo looked at his assorted crew. "You guys okay with that?"

They looked at each other. Some shrugged. Others nodded. One by one they filed back out. Nice try, Mateo. It should have made Joseph smile, but it didn't. He didn't care anymore. Not until Baba decided whether he and Maman were going to Israel. He didn't want to go. He didn't want to stay.

His swollen cheek throbbed. He had a splitting headache. His ribs hurt so badly that he was glad to just sit and not have to move. It was against the rules to sleep during detention, but that was all that Joseph wanted to do. He slouched into his desk like Larry and looked sightlessly at the book in front of him. Larry was someone to learn from. He'd had lots of experience.

35
CAPPED

Joseph sat in algebra class drawing an F-15E Strike Eagle fighter jet on the paper cover of his math book. Like him, the jet was stuck to a book. The PA system crackled. Mr. Lamb announced a special assembly. When the bell rang, students were to proceed immediately to the gym. Joseph couldn't imagine what for. Mateo usually gave him advance notice when there was something going on. When he climbed the bleachers to his homeroom section with Roberto and Alex, Joseph looked around. Mateo stood next to Mr. Lamb. Whatever it was, Mateo was part of it.

The band was on the gym floor, but they weren't playing anything. They usually knew what was going on. Anyone who was going to sink his braces into a clarinet reed deserved to know why. Even the teachers shrugged when asked thirty million times what was going on.

Once everyone was seated, Mateo went to the lectern. Mateo tapped the microphone a couple of times. He took some note cards from his shirt pocket. "What's going on?" Joseph asked Roberto.

"Don't know. Probably some dumbass project he thinks will make Hazel a model city," said Roberto.

"Good afternoon staff and students," Mateo said. "Thank you for coming."

As if anyone there had a choice. *Evening news or football, son?* Joseph didn't care, though. He had one more day of detention, and then he could start going to basketball practice again. Even that wasn't particularly motivating. He still felt Baba's threat of a move even though Baba had not mentioned it again. His red-and-purple ribs still hurt badly. Mrs. Draper should take a look at that simple misunderstanding.

"Today I want to talk about Texas history," said Mateo, "and how each one of us can be part of it."

Roberto was right. It was likely some stupid fundraising program. Joseph really didn't feel like washing cars or selling candy so they could build a new wing of the public library with more black-and-white photographs of the Alamo decorating the walls.

Mateo continued, "The first Texans in this area were the Caddo, Apache, Comanche, Wichita, and Tonkawa. They were killed or pushed onto reservations by European settlers."

That wasn't exactly news.

"A lot of Hispanics in Texas are descended from the Basque, a Spanish people that I could find nowhere in our social studies textbooks. And I checked the sixth-, seventh-, and eighth-grade textbooks."

Of course he did.

Mateo went on, "The Basque are a warrior people with

their own language. Many of them immigrated to the New World because of persecution in Spain, like many Jews. They were attracted to Tejas because they were expert ranchers and horsemen. My papá is still a proud vaquero. He's proud of our Basque heritage, but he loves Texas. Texas is our home. Many of the Tejanos had Basque blood, including those who fought at the Alamo. They fought alongside Texans and fighters who came from other places to defend the Republic of Texas."

Yep. Probably a fundraiser for more pictures, replicas, and sculptures of the Alamo.

Mateo pushed the note cards away. "We have seen upsetting things on television. Americans have been taken hostage in a foreign country. It is humiliating. It is frustrating. We do not understand the language, the culture, or the religion of the hostage takers. For the most part, we don't want to. We are just upset that Americans are seen as weak. We want to kill everyone in the Middle East. I've heard the talk. And you know, I'm upset, too."

A low murmur of agreement went through the gym. Gee, thanks, Mateo. Good lookin' out, friend.

Mateo continued, "But to attack someone whose parents emigrated from that country is plain stupid."

Okay, that stopped the murmuring. Stopped it cold. It wasn't a friendly cold, though.

"I don't know any Iranians. Or Muslims. I don't know anyone who works in the US Embassy, either. I don't know the president of the United States. I don't even know a real Basque or Spaniard." Mateo looked around. From the sixth-grade bleachers to the seventh grade to the eighth grade. "But I do know an American. A Texan whose parents left Iran to find a better life here like my Basque great-great-great-grandparents. Probably like your great-great-great-grandparents. The ones who weren't really the first Texans. That Texan I'm talking about is my best friend."

Something inside of Joseph flipped. Mateo thought Joseph was his best friend? Joseph thought Mateo only tolerated him because he kept Roberto busy.

Mateo continued, "That Texan stands for the national anthem. He pledges allegiance to the flag of the United States of America. He's a math nerd, but he'll help anyone with their homework, including me. He can sing the University of Texas fight song. He plays on our basketball team. From what I hear, the high school coaches are very anxious for him to be on the football team next year. He's as Texan and American as anyone in this gym. You all know him. He and my brother are always walking around with little grins on their faces. It's usually because they're up to something. I'm not saying I know who put the Out of Order sign on the teachers' restroom or the plate of Oreos with toothpaste filling in the coaches' office, but I have my suspicions."

There was a low wave of affirming snickers.

Mateo looked over at Mr. Lamb and said, "If I were you, I'd check beneath my office chair every now and then. I've heard that if you tape an airhorn beneath the seat, it doesn't take much pressure to make it go off."

Mr. Lamb's big eyes opened bigger, and the students howled. Roberto and Joseph ducked their heads low. Mateo paused, collected his note cards, and stuck them in a shirt pocket. "You guys elected me president of the student council. I am very proud to be the first Spanish-speaking student elected in school history. I believe in our school, but after the things that have happened over the last week, I think we need more Out of Order signs."

An uneasy murmur swept across the gym.

"So now," said Mateo, "Mr. Lamb has given me permission to dismiss this assembly my way. If you are proud of this school and believe that every single student has a right to be here regardless of where his parents were born, then remain in your seats. If you think you are better than anyone else based on where you were born or who your parents are, then please, get up and leave now. You are dismissed to go back to class."

The uneasy murmur ceased, and this time the silence was so heavy that the hum of the gym lights was nearly deafening. Joseph looked around, and so did Roberto. No one moved. Not one single student stood. The band students didn't even fidget. Mateo took his time, sweeping his eyes back and forth across the gym twice.

"So today," said Mateo, "the Fighting Hawks have spoken. I am proud of the students I represent. I believe in this school, its students, its teachers, and the staff. This is a moment that we will all look back on, and we will be proud of one another. Go Hawks. Fly high." Mateo turned and nodded to the band teacher, who stood and gave the signal to the band. With a half turn, Mateo faced the big American flag hanging on the gym wall, and the band played the national anthem.

Joseph stood, put his hand over his heart, and fought to sort his emotions, but it wasn't easy. The band followed with the school fight song. The energy of the song eased the catch in his throat and that horrible feeling of the whole school looking at him. That the whole school was there because of him. Yeah, Joseph's best friend would be governor of Texas someday.

Everyone knew Joseph had been jumped. Everyone knew he didn't snitch. He'd gone to detention for a week without complaining. Now there was no more trash in his locker, no more names shouted in the hallway, and the trashing of their yard gradually stopped. Kids now smiled at him, even some that were friends with the Posse. They didn't think of it all by themselves, though. It took Mateo shaming them into it. Why did it take something that drastic? Although it was a relief, Joseph just tried not to think about it.

36
THE DROP OF A HAT

One morning, Joseph made prayers with Baba in his study. Maman made a huge breakfast to celebrate Baba's long weekend home. After prayers, Baba took the time to go over Joseph's investment statement with him. Together they double-checked the mathematics. When Baba placed Joseph's statement in the office safe with his own, Joseph saw something interesting inside.

Something was wrapped in a long, thick, silklike pouch. The fabric looked very old. "What is that?" asked Joseph.

Baba removed the pouch and placed it on the desk. He opened it and withdrew a long, rectangular knife. "It's a *shechita* knife, one of the few things I was able to carry out of Iran. It is for slaughtering an animal according to kosher laws. It's been in our family for many generations. We had to leave Iran quickly. There was little that Maman and I could take but a small bag apiece. She was able to bring the silver Shabbat candlesticks and the silver matchbook holder. I took the knife, my tallit, and tefillin. I never dreamed that . . ." Baba's voice drifted off, like Maman's did sometimes when she spoke of Iran.

When they spoke of the food, the holidays, and trips to the countryside, they spoke with longing. When their actual exit came up, neither would say exactly what happened. Secret police. Safer.

"Why did you have to leave, Baba?"

"Someone who was jealous of my position with the National Iranian Oil Company told a lie. They said I was selling information about the Iranian oil operations to Western countries. Those countries bought Iranian oil cheap, but they sold back petroleum products to Iran at ridiculously high prices. The Shah needed those products to modernize the country, but the Western companies controlled the markets. Iran could never profit from its own oil."

Well, unless it was lost in Uncle Eli's dessert rant, that was more than Joseph had ever heard before. "What happened?" asked Joseph.

"I wasn't the one who was doing it. It was a family member . . ."

"Who?" Joseph interrupted.

There was a long silence, and then Baba said barely above a whisper, "Your uncle. Your maman's brother."

"The one who was killed in a bomb in Israel?"

"Yes. You must never tell this to anyone, Joseph. Promise me. And never mention it to Maman."

"Yes, sir. But didn't Maman's brother and his family live in California, too?"

"Yes. The British and Israelis helped his family escape from the Shah's secret police. They set them up to live in California.

No one helped your maman and me, though. Without a Muslim neighbor in Tehran and some Christians who lived in the mountains, we'd have never made it to Turkey. I'd set aside a little money in a bank in England when I was in college there. I put a bit more in there from time to time to keep the account active once I went back to Iran and started working. From Turkey, we used the last of our money to fly to London. It took almost everything in the England account to live while we waited for visas to the United States."

Compared to anything Joseph had heard up until now, it was a gold mine of information. "Baba, are the secret police still looking for you?"

"We don't know, Youssef-jun. We thought they would settle for chasing us out of the country, but then what happened to your uncle and aunt . . . a bomb. It could have been a terrorist act, or they could have been targeted. I could never find good work in California, so I found a job with an oil company here in Texas. We moved away from the Persian community in Los Angeles. In California, I worked two janitorial jobs and cleaned the synagogue, but it simply wasn't enough money to live on. We've had no trouble since we moved here, but it's hard living in a place where we are separated from our own people and language."

As the darkness gave way to the grayness of dawn outside the window, a little light shined into Joseph's understanding. Baba was college educated, a gentleman to all, a man who minded his own business. The thought of his father mopping floors and cleaning synagogue toilets because of the Shah's police sparked Joseph's indignation. Baba was never bitter, though. He simply did what he had to do to earn for his family. Like

LaLa said, wearing Kamran Nissan's hat was earned through bearing burdens.

It made more sense now. If what had happened to them since the American diplomats had been taken hostage was "no trouble" to Baba, what he thought the secret police might do must be really bad. That must be why Maman didn't want the Shah of Iran here. She feared his security team might still look for them.

"The Shah's police are that upset about oil?" asked Joseph.

Baba made a vague murmur that could have meant anything.

"Why didn't Shahla come with us?" asked Joseph.

Baba glanced away, maybe concealing an expression. "It was Shahla's father who caused all our troubles, Youssef. You have to understand, this all happened many years ago. Wounds were fresh. I should have taken her in, but I was afraid for you and her when I heard that it was a bomb. Maybe it was random, maybe it wasn't. At the time, it made sense to divide in order to protect. Your maman couldn't bear not to see her brother's child, though, and it hasn't really worked. When I realized how much it hurt your maman, Shahla had already adjusted to life with her adoptive parents. Her adoptive parents are old and childless, and she is the light of their eyes. It would be cruel to her and them to take her away."

"Oh," said Joseph.

It still seemed very anti-Persian to him. This reflected in his tone, because Baba said, "I know it seems foolish now, Youssef, but we all make foolish decisions when we're afraid, sad, and angry. Just promise me that you'll always look after Shahla like she's your sister. Even though she's far away, protect her and love her however you can. She feels the rejection deeply."

"I know," said Joseph.

37
HAT TRICK

"Can I borrow your helmet and jacket?" Joseph asked Roberto.

"Why?"

Joseph told him.

"Dude, you so gonna get in trouble."

"So can I?"

"Sure."

The place Joseph had in mind was an abandoned farm. It was mostly pastureland, but there were lots of trees around the house. The trees nearly swallowed the old house like a disenchanted forest. He and Roberto sometimes went fishing in the big pond at the back of the property. Joseph didn't much care for fishing. Roberto thought that threading sticky, slimy worms onto a hook and waiting for an equally slimy fish to take the bait was an essential Texas skill. The fishing was okay. It was the waiting on the bank with wasps, spiders, ants, and ticks that Joseph didn't like. Only one living creature at a time needed to be inside his clothes, and Joseph was

the one. He didn't like extra creatures conducting coloniza-
tion explorations.

Joseph would execute his plan in the daytime, so he needed
a disguise.

The real treasure of the abandoned farm perched in the
overgrown oak trees behind the house: a tree house. With a bit
of repair work on some rotting edges and renailing the strips of
wood that served as rungs, Roberto and Joseph found it quite
cozy. They put two old stools from Mr. Ybarra's workshop up
there to use as tables. When they tired of fishing, they played
cards in the tree house.

They stashed two fishing poles, a tackle box, and a flashlight
up there. Joseph wanted to show the tree house to Vonda. For
once they could talk without a hundred people around. People
who might tell Reverend Baer that Vonda was with the skinny
Jewish boy from Eye-ran.

They set up their date for when Vonda's parents went on
the annual trip to Waco for a pastors' retreat. One of her sisters
who went to a religious college in Oklahoma was coming home
for the weekend to stay with Vonda. She would be more interested in catching up with high school friends, wrote Vonda, and
not likely to say anything about Vonda going out for a while.

When Joseph and Baba returned from their Sunday morning flying lessons, Joseph told Baba that he was going to take
out his dirt bike. Baba usually fell asleep in his recliner while
Maman did his laundry and repacked his work bag for the week.

Joseph took an early trip to the tree house to clean and make
everything ready. Afterward, he rode his dirt bike as quietly as
he could through Hazel's Sunday silence. He turned into the
alley behind the 7-11, which really was open from 7:00 a.m. to

11:00 p.m. for seven days per week. Traffic there was normal. Vonda was already in the alley when Joseph rolled up, and he handed her Roberto's jacket and helmet. With a little adjustment and help with where to put her feet, she snuggled behind Joseph and gripped him around his waist.

There was a Hafiz-like poetry in her closeness. Joseph had only experienced that in little thrills during their brief touches over a math problem or a piano lesson. Now something flooded through him that was indescribably joyful. Resisting the urge to peel out and show her all his skill, to release the excitement bubbling everywhere inside him, Joseph forced himself to putter through town until he reached the city limits.

From there, Joseph opened the throttle and said over his shoulder, "Hang on!"

Vonda's grip tightened. She scooted even closer. They skimmed the roadside, nosed into ditches, and jumped small hills. They made tight turns and wound through paths that wormed through the mesquite, squatty oaks, and scrub pine. Joseph was showing off, but he didn't care. For too long Vonda had remained beyond his reach. He wanted to show her more than some chords on the piano, more than a nice haircut, more than a math problem, more than getting beat up in the hallway and sitting with the losers in detention.

Joseph would have kept going, but they had limited time. He wanted to make sure they had time at the tree house. He wasn't sure if girls liked tree houses, but he'd dressed it up as much as he could: a spare blanket that Maman would never miss; Baba's old handkerchiefs for cloths to cover the stool-tables; some packages of Little Debbies that LaLa didn't begrudge him; a yellow rose from Maman's Shabbat bouquet; a can of mixed nuts left over from his bar mitzvah; two Coca-Colas that wouldn't be cold.

He wrapped his greatest gift in glittery, star-blue wrapping paper and silver ribbon that he'd saved from a Hanukkah present. Joseph placed it on her cushion, propping it there carefully like it was in a window display. It was his black-and-gold home football jersey, freshly laundered and folded neatly like a new dress shirt.

Joseph pulled into the driveway of the abandoned farmhouse. When he found the spot where he and Roberto usually stashed their dirt bikes, he cut the engine and removed his helmet. Vonda stepped off, and Joseph laid the bike on the ground to keep it out of sight. With all the tender care he could muster, he helped her unsnap the chin strap, remove the helmet, and straighten her hair. Her hair was so golden, so soft like he'd imagined. Even tousled, it looked good. Natural.

"That was fun," she said a little breathlessly.

"I want to take you flying someday," said Joseph, "when I get my pilot's license. We can fly over Eagle Mountain Lake."

"I doubt we'd slip that one by Reverend Charles Baer," said Vonda wryly.

"Ready to see your surprise?"

Vonda nodded. Joseph took her by the hand. He showed her the wooden rungs that led up to the tree house. They blended with the camouflage of split bark on the blackjack oaks.

"Wow," she said. "Are you sure it's okay to be out here?"

"We've never seen a soul out here but us," said Joseph.

"Who's 'us'?"

"Roberto and me. Sometimes Alex. Mateo likes to read up here."

"Oh."

"You want to go first?" asked Joseph.

"Okay." Vonda still had that look that drove him crazy, but it was only barely there. She showed a genuine curiosity in what lay above the branches. She climbed. Joseph climbed behind her.

Vonda walked around the tree house, inspecting it while Joseph pointed out the pond in the far distance and a few other points of interest. There wasn't much to see but brown fields. "In the spring, it's a lot nicer," said Joseph. "Right now, it's only a few pines that are green, but when the oaks turn green, it's like being in a big, leafy cloud up here."

"I'd like to see it in the spring, then," said Vonda, leaning out of the window to look below. Joseph moved closer beside her and put his arm around her. They stood for several seconds watching the chilly breeze stir the high, dead grass below. She was shorter than Joseph, so his arm felt natural around her shoulder.

"Are you cold?" he asked, pulling her closer and savoring the soft curve of her hip against him. "I have a blanket."

"No, I'm comfortable," she said. "Roberto's jacket kept me toasty."

Joseph wondered how his body felt to her. He had decent abs. His arms were strong even though his muscles weren't bulky like Larry's and Juan's. Did girls like flat stomachs? He had a flat stomach. Vonda had complimented him one time on his eyes. She said his lashes were so long and dark that it looked like he wore mascara. Having suffered through way too many "Pretty Boys" in the locker room, Joseph wasn't sure long eyelashes were a real selling point.

Her hair smelled like green apples. That reminded Joseph of a line of poetry.

"'I want to do with you what spring does to the cherry trees,'" said Joseph softly.

Vonda blushed deeply. "What do you mean by that?"

"It worked," said Joseph, turning her to him. He touched his fingers tenderly to her left cheek. "Your cheeks bloomed."

"Oh," she said.

Her cheek was so soft, even softer than her hands. Joseph cupped her left cheek more firmly in his right palm, bent, and kissed her softly on the lips. He drew away and looked into those star-blue eyes. "Like that. Your whole face is . . . beautiful. Like spring."

She blushed even more deeply and looked down. Right here, right now was where Joseph had wanted to be since they played the duet on LaLa's piano bench.

Suddenly, she took his hand. "Joseph, look," said Vonda. "You and I . . . this will never work like you want it to. My father will never let me . . . let us . . . unless you were Christian. But even then, we're too young. My father won't let me date at all. It's not just you."

"Why not?" asked Joseph. "My parents won't let me date, either, but we can . . ."

"No," said Vonda. "We can't. Someone will eventually tell my father. I know you think he's an awful man, but there's a reason he watches me so closely."

"What is it?" asked Joseph.

"My oldest sister . . . something bad happened."

"What?"

"She . . . Joseph, you can't tell anyone. Swear to me."

"I swear."

"She got pregnant her senior year in high school. They sent her away to a girls home where they'd take care of her until the baby came. The deal was that she had to put the baby up for adoption. She really didn't want to. It was a shame to our family, especially our father. He'd have to give up the ministry if people found out. She wasn't right after she gave up the baby. Exactly six weeks after my sister turned over the baby to the agency, she killed herself."

"Geez," said Joseph. "I don't even know what to say to that. I'm so sorry for you. Were you close?"

"Not really. She was seven years older than me. She and my father were close until he found out she was pregnant. After that, it was nothing but fighting," said Vonda.

"That must have been recent," said Joseph, calculating ages in his head.

"Yeah," said Vonda. "It's made things hard around the house and at the church. It's a small town, and small town people talk. Daddy makes up for it by being as strict as he can with everyone. It's how you get back in everyone's good graces, I guess. We don't know if anyone knows about the pregnancy, but a child who commits suicide? Not kosher."

"Kosher?" asked Joseph.

"Oh, I'm sorry," said Vonda. "Around here it means, like, acceptable, you know?"

"Well, that's what it means," said Joseph, "but it usually applies to food."

"So you're not offended we can't be together?"

"I'm sad," said Joseph. "I'm not sure I know the difference between offended and sad. I don't understand."

"Don't be sad, Joseph. Dad will never stop being strict about home and Mom and the Ten Commandments and apple pie and no-foreigners-better-insult-the-flag and all that. It's how he keeps his dignity."

"Can we even be friends?" asked Joseph. His heart wasn't sinking. It was slamming its fist into his chest and abdomen, grabbing his throat, desperately trying to find a place to reconnect, but Vonda had become withdrawn. Why had she let him get this close and then pushed him away?

"No."

There was a long silence, and Joseph turned and looked at the table he'd carefully set for her arrival. "No notes?"

"It would just make it harder on both of us."

"You knew this from the beginning," said Joseph. "You knew and you didn't tell me. You planned this day to tell me goodbye."

"I'm sorry."

"But you're not sad?" asked Joseph.

"Yes, I'm sad," said Vonda. "But we have to stop."

"Why?"

"I just told you."

Joseph stared at her, and she stared back. Her face was unreadable when she wanted it to be. And it was. Maybe there was a hint of shininess in her eyes, maybe not. "Could we talk about this?" he asked. He was begging. He knew it.

"Can you please take me home?"

The ride back to town was so cold that they could have wedged the Coca-Colas between them and brought them to perfect, refrigerated frostiness. Vonda's hands around his waist were so light. Joseph remained stiff in her grip. Blue-eyed Canon. Rage. Control. Rage. Control. How do you survive a fall from a tree house?

LaLa could probably help him understand what just happened, but Joseph was sick of life lessons and word games. No matter where he turned, life was out of control.

38
HATS OFF

The police came while Joseph and Baba were praying afternoon prayers on Shabbat.

Baba and Joseph heard the doorbell, but prayers were not to be interrupted. They continued together: "Blessed are You, HaShem, Who blesses His people Israel with peace. My God, keep my tongue from evil and my lips from speaking deceitfully . . ."

"Kamran!" called Maman from the front of the house.

The alarm in Maman's voice made them both pause. She wouldn't interrupt if it weren't important. Maman rarely raised her voice.

"Kamran!" she said again. Her voice was closer. Maman's footsteps were usually light. Not today. The urgency in her voice matched her footsteps on the wooden floor. Miss LaNell's high heels would have lost a marching match with Maman today.

Baba and Joseph turned as she paused at Baba's office door.

"Police."

Oh, no. Joseph looked up at Baba. Had Reverend Baer called the police on him for taking Vonda riding on his dirt bike? Did he know they'd kissed? Baba paled, but he kissed his prayer book reverently and placed it on the table. Joseph did the same. They followed Maman back down the hall to the living room.

The front door was open, but the screen door was closed. Two men in suits and a uniformed officer stood on the porch looking around. Baba walked to the door. "I can help you?" he asked.

"Mr. Nissan?" asked the uniformed officer.

"I'm Kamran Nissan," said Baba.

"May we come in for a moment?" asked the uniformed officer. "This is our local city detective, Paul White, and Dallas city police detective, Troy Bender. I'm James Oliver." Joseph recognized Officer Oliver. He worked security at the junior high football and basketball games. He spent a lot more time watching the games than the crowds, probably because his son played on the football team.

There was a long silence. Joseph could see the war in Baba's face. Wordlessly, Baba extended his hand and pushed open the screen. The three policemen came inside, each looking around. When their eyes came to rest on Joseph, each expression relaxed. Like one does when he's found something he's looking for. "Aren't you Joseph?" asked Officer Oliver.

"I am Joseph."

Detective White asked Baba, "Would you and your son mind coming down to the police department with us? We have some questions we'd like to ask you about a case we're working on."

"We can't," said Baba.

"Are you busy?" asked Officer Oliver, looking around the quiet house.

"It's Shabbat," said Baba.

"It's Shab-what?" said Detective White.

"Shabbat," repeated Detective Bender. "They're Jewish, remember? They don't drive on their Sabbath."

Baba removed the prayer shawl and handed it to Joseph. "Please go put this in my study, Youssef."

Joseph took the familiar tallit. It was still warm from body heat. He took it back to the study, folded it, and put it on Baba's desk. He then did the same with his bar mitzvah tallit. When he walked back down the hallway, he heard the voices moving to the dining room.

Baba seated them around the dining table. The three men looked at the white Shabbat tablecloth, candlesticks, and the remains of the challah bread. Officer Oliver also sat. If they'd brought him to arrest Joseph, he wasn't doing it immediately.

"Youssef, sit," said Baba in English. "Answer them the questions."

Joseph sat, wondering how much the policemen knew. The less he said, the better.

Maman entered with a large silver tray of almond cookies, teacups, teabags, and a teapot full of hot water. Joseph tried not to frown. Maman was about to give these men the last of the Shabbat cookies. Of course, if he was going to jail, it didn't really matter. He'd get bread and water. Or maybe meals all seasoned with cafeteria tomato sauce.

Maman set the tray down, poured the hot water for each teacup, and turned to leave the room. Detective White said, "Ma'am, please stay. We'd like to hear from you, too."

Baba lifted his chin in an angry motion that dismissed her. "Why . . . ?" asked Detective White.

Joseph better explain, or they'd drag Maman into this. Then Baba would really kill him. "It's impolite," said Joseph to the detective.

"I don't understand," said Detective White.

"They're from Iran. It's impolite to ask a Persian man about his wife or daughters or speak to them directly if you're not part of the family. It's kind of . . ." How would his wedgy social studies teacher put it? "It's a cultural thing. Men deal with public life, and women take care of the home stuff. You're public. That's the best I can explain it."

Detective Bender nodded as if he understood. Maybe since he was from Dallas, he dealt more with other ethnic groups.

Detective White looked less sure. "So did I get your mother in trouble . . . ?"

"No. Baba doesn't get angry with her. It only looks that way. He's . . . well . . . he's just . . . Persian. He's saving face."

Officer Oliver grinned at Detective White and translated into Texan: "That's his woman. Like you don't go up to a roughneck's woman in a bar and buy her a drink."

"Oh," said Detective White, as if that made perfect sense and they were all now one big, happy Texiranian family.

Detective Bender took a polite sip of his tea. So far, no one had touched the cookies. There was hope. Joseph wasn't in handcuffs yet, and the cookies were undisturbed.

Detective White fished some photos out of his suit coat pocket. "Joseph, the Hazel Police Department and Sheriff's Office are cooperating with Tarrant County Police Department. They are investigating a drug ring in Dallas. Since back in the fall, we've had a location here in our county under surveillance. We believe that it is a way station for a drug supply chain from Mexico. Do you recognize this location?" He put a photograph in front of Joseph. It was the barn where he and Roberto had seen the Edmondsons.

Joseph looked at Baba, who nodded. "Tell the truth," he said.

My God, keep my tongue from evil and my lips from speaking deceitfully. Was it possible to do both at the same time? "Yes, sir," said Joseph to Detective White.

"We haven't been able to find any evidence to submit to the local judge to obtain a search warrant for the barn property. The owner of the property next to it gave us permission to search the fence line. There's a creek bed between the properties. Does this look familiar?" He placed a couple more photographs on the table. One was the gap in the fence where he and Roberto had ridden through. The other was of the dirt mounds. Dirt mounds full of dirt bike tracks.

Joseph nodded.

Detective Bender spoke next. "Drug runners don't jump dirt bikes in their spare time. Detective White called in our forensics expert from Dallas. He did some analysis on the tracks. In the meantime, Detective White did some asking around. It seems that the Ybarra boys and the Nissan boy are usually together on dirt bikes. There are three sets of dirt bike tracks leading up to the property. Only two continued onto it and were ridden on the dirt mounds. What happened with them after that was a little confusing, but it was the same two bikes."

Good grief. Did these detectives think Joseph and Roberto were drug dealers? This was worse than getting caught with

Vonda. Drug dealers went to prison, not religious school in Israel. Joseph thought he'd pass out.

"You are frighting him. Please make to the point," said Baba.

"The Ybarra twins and their father came down to the station this morning and spoke with us. They admitted that they own the two dirt bikes that made these tracks. What we need to know," said Detective Bender, "is whether you and Roberto saw anything while you were out there. Anything strange. People. Vehicles."

"What did Roberto say?" asked Joseph.

"What's important is what you say," said Detective White.

Joseph fell silent. If he told, he would be in trouble for more than trespassing. He and Roberto knew of a crime and didn't report it. He was pretty sure that was a crime, too. A prison crime. No wonder Baba was afraid of the police. You could get in trouble for just knowing something.

"Look, son," said Officer Oliver. "You're not in trouble. Not at all. If you can tell us the same story Roberto told us, then we can go to the judge and obtain a warrant to search the premises. We need you to confirm what Roberto said. Don't be scared to tell the truth."

Joseph looked at Baba. "Tell the truth, Youssef," he said again. "Don't be afraid."

"Am I in trouble for trespassing?" Joseph asked Officer Oliver. Maybe they'd better clear up that part of the deal.

Officer Oliver grinned. "It would be easy to miss that posted sign."

Joseph looked at him doubtfully.

Extending his hand, Officer Oliver selected the photo of the gap in the fence line. He tapped it. "See? It doesn't show up in the photograph at all."

"But . . ."

"Son, if you tell us what you saw in that barn, I promise you that the posted sign won't be there tomorrow." He tore the picture in two and pushed it across the table to Joseph. Officer Oliver was a practical man. He'd do well bargaining in the markets in the Old City of Jerusalem.

Joseph sighed. "We saw the Edmondsons drive their old blue GMC pickup into the barn."

"Date and time?" asked Detective Bender.

Joseph gave it.

Baba glared at him.

Oy veh. There was no way Joseph was going to get out of this okay. If he survived this interview, he'd be grounded from riding his dirt bike for a month.

Joseph said, "They changed into different clothes, dressed-up cowboy clothes. Then they loaded white packages of marijuana into the toolbox of a newer truck. A big, red, shiny dually Ford. They covered it back up and drove off."

"How did you know it was marijuana?" asked Detective White.

"After they left, we sneaked inside. There was a trapdoor built into an old feed bin inside a storage room. Roberto went down the ladder. He said it was a big room, a basement. That was probably where all the dirt piles came from." Joseph leaned back in his chair. "That's all I know."

"Thank you, son," said Detective Bender. "That's enough for us to obtain a search warrant. You've been a big help."

"One more thing," said Detective White. "I've been investigating marijuana and pills sold at the high school. My sources say that most of it is actually coming from a dealer at the junior high school. Do you know anything about that?"

Joseph froze. He'd just told on Larry's and Brian's dads. They'd go to prison. If he told the detective that Brian was selling drugs at the junior high school, Brian would also go to jail. "Juvy," as the kids called it. Suddenly, Joseph had the power to make sure the Edmondsons were thoroughly punished for their bullying and for LaLa's lost groceries.

It should feel good to get them back, but it didn't. The Edmondson cousins had been kept back a grade in elementary school because their dads were in prison. Maybe Larry's mother had moved away because she needed a job or from embarrassment. Maybe she had put Larry back a grade to be with Brian, to face the embarrassment together. Larry wasn't dumb. He knew the football plays better than anyone on the team.

If Persians understood anything, it was saving face. The Edmondsons were not rich people. Larry and Brian didn't have much of a chance. They didn't have a father there to take them to a church, to help them with math, to watch their football games. Larry and Brian's fathers never came to watch. Even though Brian sold drugs, it didn't change anything. He still wore worn clothes. He still rode his old bicycle. He was still on free lunch at school. What if Brian's dad was making him sell the drugs?

Keep my lips from speaking deceitfully. Maybe it was deceitful, and maybe it wasn't.

"I don't know any drug dealers," said Joseph.

"The look on your face is telling me different," said Detective White.

"Maybe there are drug dealers at the junior high school," said Joseph. "But they're no friends of mine. You should ask someone who hangs around with that crowd. I hang out with the nerds, the jocks, and the Mexicans. Not druggies."

39
BOTTLE CAP

"Joseph."

Joseph paused in unlooping his bicycle security chain from around its frame. He looked up. It was Vonda. His heart skipped some beats. Maybe it hadn't read its typed obituary yet.

"Yeah?"

"Could you walk with me to the park? I have something I want to tell you. Something I meant to give you."

"We shouldn't," said Joseph.

"I know," said Vonda. "But I wanted to tell you how sorry I was about the Posse. You looked so awful. I should have told you at the tree house, but things moved too fast that day, and I never got to tell you. It nearly killed me not to talk to you and make sure you were okay after the fight."

"You managed."

"Joseph, please. I just want to talk for five minutes. I need to."

This time it was Joseph who merely shrugged his permission.

They walked in silence to the park. Not a touch or even an

accidental brush. Joseph walked on the street side of the side-walk. The bicycle made a barrier between them. One of the Posse walked ahead of them. Joseph wondered if Vonda were setting him up. The Posse was outlawed at school, but they could lurk around the neighborhood. The boy was the one who had insulted Larry so vilely. He kept glancing around at Joseph and Vonda until he reached his house and went inside. Thug.

They reached the park, and Joseph propped his bike against a concrete table. He turned to face Vonda.

"What?" he asked. Might as well get it over with.

"Don't hate me," she whispered.

"I don't hate you," said Joseph. "But you need to get to the point. It's not safe for you to be around me right now." Where there was one Posse boy, there could be more.

Vonda took his hand, but Joseph pulled it away. It hurt too much. Her eyes grew watery, maybe with genuine tears.

"Joseph, have you ever done something just because you had to be the grown-up for your parents? Something you didn't really want to do?" asked Vonda.

The electric shock to his heart was a real jolt. Joseph stared, wanting the feeling to die. How dare she touch that string. Pain. Control.

Vonda continued. "If you were Christian. If I were Jewish. If we were twenty years old instead of thirteen. We will never be together because our parents already have their burdens. In the end, we don't want to add to them. If my father loses his pastorate, I don't know what he'll do. When I think of my sister, I don't know what people do when they hurt so much they can't stand it. I'm not willing to find out." She took something from her jacket pocket.

"I know," said Joseph. "I get it. So can I go home now?"

Vonda extended her hand, but as she did, she looked past Joseph's shoulder. Her eyes widened in fear. What was it? The Posse? Joseph whirled to face whoever it was. Instead of a trench coat, it was Reverend Baer who strode toward him. So there it was. They were at a bottleneck. They couldn't pretend they weren't communicating. Reverend Charles Baer saw them.

"You should go," said Vonda.

"No," said Joseph. He wasn't going to start running now. He'd rather take a tongue-lashing than end up like Baba, hiding from everything because of the authorities. Let Reverend Heavenly Authority himself bring it on.

It took over a minute for Reverend Baer to cross the street and make it to the picnic table, though. Joseph had so many second thoughts during the long wait that the second thoughts added up to well over a dozen. He was afraid, but determination finally turned the anxious jelly in his stomach to iron. It steeled his ribs, which throbbed in anticipation. When Reverend Baer reached them, Joseph had no fear at all. He was empty of anything.

"Daddy, no . . ." pled Vonda. The reverend closed the last few yards of the distance between them. In the fraction of a second before Reverend Baer shoved him, Joseph knew who snitched. The Posse boy had called ahead to the parsonage or church office and told on them.

The shove was hard. Joseph stumbled backward, knocking his bicycle down with him. He landed half on the brown grass and half on the concrete pad. It hurt, but not too much. There wasn't much that hurt worse than a lock in a sock. Before he could disentangle himself from the bike and get back to his feet, the reverend unleashed a storm of hateful words at Joseph. It was so severe that Vonda interrupted, "Daddy, no, it's my fault. I asked him . . ."

"Shut up and go home, Vonda," said Reverend Baer. He kicked hard toward Joseph, catching the rear bicycle tire.

Whatever she wanted to say back, Vonda capped it tightly. "Sorry," she mouthed to Joseph. She put something back in her pocket and walked toward home.

The rant resumed, and Joseph separated himself from the bike and stood. He faced Reverend Baer. His jacket was torn. Oddly, this angered Joseph worse than being shoved. Rage. Control. Vonda leaving him alone to face her father angered Joseph worse than being shoved. Rage. Control.

When the shouting stopped, or at least when the man took a breath, Joseph lifted his bicycle and said, "Six hundred and thirteen."

"What?" asked the reverend.

"Six hundred and thirteen," said Joseph. "There are six hundred and thirteen commandments, not ten. Every Jewish second grader knows that. And every Jewish second grader knows you don't push people around who didn't do anything to you. You don't damage other people's property. You should know that even if you only know the ten. Your Bible's bigger than mine."

For once, Reverend Charles Baer was speechless. Joseph rode away. The bicycle chain rubbed a metallic, grinding rhythm against the bent derailleur.

40

CYCLING HELMET

Joseph had cut and scraped his hand deeply in breaking the fall. He thought of going to LaLa's first so she could clean the cut and put a Band-Aid on it before Maman saw it. LaLa had first-aid spray that didn't sting as bad. Really, he just missed LaLa, but he didn't want to involve her in another transgression. He'd take his chances at home. Maman quizzed him about it at supper. Joseph said he fell down with his bike. Next came that stinging orange stuff and a Band-Aid.

Maman noticed Joseph's dark mood, but since all the trouble started, she'd questioned him less and consulted him more. He'd just keep it to himself. No sense in worrying about Maman picking up the poker to visit a church for the first time in her life. Baba didn't say much about the hand on Friday evening. He was more concerned about getting to the apartment to prepare for Friday-evening synagogue service. After the Shabbat afternoon nap on Saturday, Joseph walked with Baba back to the synagogue for concluding prayers. On the walk back to the apartment, Baba asked.

"I fell with my bike, Baba," said Joseph.

"Youssef, your English is better than mine," said Baba. "Tell me what happened. Americans don't fall with their bikes. They wreck their bikes."

So Joseph told. And Joseph waited for the rebuke. He knew he shouldn't have walked to the park with Vonda. He should have walked away. But there was no rebuke. There was only a frown of sadness. Baba placed his hand atop Joseph's kippah in a gesture of comfort. They walked like that for several strides. Joseph felt his father's helplessness match his own.

Joseph wanted to stop and wrap his arms around Baba, to be comforted or even gently scolded like when he was little. Instead, Baba left Joseph to sort out his questions, anger, and disappointments as they walked. Baba finally spoke.

"Joseph, you will marry a Jewish woman. There's no point in becoming emotional about a girl who isn't." He said it with such finality. "You're too young to be so serious about a girl. When it's time to marry, then you can allow your heart to open. Your maman was barely sixteen when we married," said Baba. "Barely more than a child. Americans marry when they're older. Hold on to your heart."

"Why did she marry so young?" asked Joseph.

"Girls married younger back then," said Baba.

Joseph asked, "How did you meet?"

"Our parents arranged it. My family went to her family's home. She served us tea and sweets. She was so very beautiful. Big, dark eyes and the blackest hair. You have her lips, Youssef, so red and perfect. Persian women are very modest, but when she served me tea, she looked me directly in the eye. I liked her fire even though I knew that was why we were matched."

"I don't understand," said Joseph. "Maman's almost always calm." It was better to keep the bareheaded, fireplace-poker-wielding, cursing Maman to himself.

"Her brothers were known for having fiery tempers. This was not safe for a Jew in any nation, much less a Jewish woman. Her family wanted her to marry into a more conservative family. Our family always have been doctors, engineers, scholars. I had returned to Tehran from England with an engineering degree. It was time to marry. I liked her instantly, but I think she was daring me not to." Baba laughed softly, something he rarely did. "You inherited her temper."

Joseph said, "Maman isn't hot-tempered, Baba. The only time I've seen her really angry was when the Shah came to America and when people trashed the yard. Anybody would get angry about that."

"Not now," agreed Baba. "Life has broken her many times. Now it's you she lives for. You're the light of her eyes."

"How did life break her?" asked Joseph.

"She tried so long to get pregnant in Iran. She miscarried several times. I was often gone working. She was alone during much of the grief." Baba's eyes moistened. "And then we lost everything because of her brother. He nearly got us killed. She took it personally even though I never blamed her." Baba paused, pain shadowing his face. "We were respected in the Jewish community in Tehran. When we moved to California, I was reduced to cleaning other people's toilets. It hurt her dignity. Her brother and sister-in-law were killed in the car bomb. And I hurt her. So when she had you, you were her redemption from all the suffering. Suffering changed her. You'd have liked to know her before . . ."

Joseph waited, but Baba didn't finish.

"How did you hurt her, Baba?"

"God has saved all her tears in a bottle, Youssef. They will testify against me someday."

Maybe the hurt Baba was talking about was not letting Maman adopt Shahla. Maman was Shahla's closest kin. She was the logical choice, not strangers.

Joseph felt like he was translating again. He was sorting through what was Iranian, what was Jewish, what was American, and what was Texan to make sense of what people were doing. Did every kid have to do this? To figure out the world around him against who he is, where he was born, and where his parents were born? Probably not.

41
PILLBOX HAT

Now that Joseph played with the basketball team, he improved his pickup games at the park. He couldn't play in Saturday tournaments, but he started every other game. His muscles started showing like the other eighth graders. Larry's masculine shape was no longer something to be envied. One time Joseph lingered before running out to the gym for practice. Larry was the only one left in the locker room. "Why?" Joseph asked. He didn't have to say what.

Larry looked at him with eyes more careworn than Baba's. He said, "Fly high or die. Hawks stick together. You go down swinging, kid." And that was it.

The team was what meant something to Larry. Like when Coach put Joseph in the game for the first time at tight end. Larry had assured Joseph that he could make the catch. The team was Larry's family.

As his father's court case dragged on, Larry's basketball skills suffered. He'd always worn his hair a little long. Now it fell below his shoulders. He smelled strongly of cigarettes. His eyes were often bloodshot. He missed shots and made bad passes. The coaches benched him. He missed some practices. When the grades posted in early March, Larry was dropped from the team. He disappeared from school a week later. The truant officer was looking for him, but no one answered at their house.

Brian still came to school. He stayed with the druggies and no longer hung out with the jocks. Last-period gym class was reserved for athletes, so Brian's gym period was changed after football season. Joseph rarely saw him.

At one of the home games, Joseph dressed out in the locker room. He remembered that he needed his Texas history book to finish his homework assignment. He'd already made enough Texas history with Mrs. Draper. He had to keep his grade up. "Tell Coach I had to run to my locker to get my history book," Joseph asked a teammate. He trotted through the long hallway toward the classrooms. When he turned the next corner, he pulled up short.

Mr. Lamb, Detective White, and a uniformed officer with a German Shepherd on a leash stood in the hallway. Brian stood to the side, head down, pockets hanging inside out. The policeman searched the open locker. Mr. Lamb looked Joseph's way.

"You can't be in the hallway right now, son," called Mr. Lamb. "Go back to the gym."

Joseph eased back. He felt exceedingly sad.

That night, Joseph said the bedtime prayer. It was the first time since the peach sharbet incident that he could be sincere.

"Master of the Universe, I forgive anyone who angered me or sinned against me. Whether it was against my body, my possessions, my honor, or against anything of mine. Whether he did it

accidentally, willfully, carelessly, or purposely. Whether he did it through words, actions, thoughts, I forgive . . ."

Why pray? Did you just keep saying the words until they were true? If so, then prayer didn't change anyone else. It changed the one saying the prayer. Like a translator.

"May no person be punished because of me."

Joseph meant it. He didn't want Brian or Larry to be punished because of him. It felt as though his hatred had somehow caused their misfortune. Joseph's logical mind told him he couldn't have been the one that caused the misfortune any more than there were chainsaw murderers and boos on the street after dark in Hazel, Texas. Still, the power of his hatred scared Joseph.

"Whatever sins I have done, may You erase them in Your great mercy, but not through any suffering or sicknesses."

What was sin? The Torah commanded people to love their fellow human beings. The Jewish sages said it summed up every law in the Bible. Joseph loved Vonda. He loved Mateo and Roberto. He loved Maman and Baba. He loved LaLa and Shahla. You couldn't be around Persians without hearing "I love you" a thousand times. Was sin *not* to love people? That made sin a big deal. And if so, then hating them was a bigger sin. Joseph now saw the reason the Edmondsons had strutted around and played football. It was the only way they'd ever be accepted or admired. Like him, they wanted to fit in.

"May the words of my mouth and the thoughts of my heart find grace before You, God."

Maybe he'd better watch the curse words, too. Mateo always said if you wanted people to listen to you, they should believe you have something to say. People liked Roberto, but they *listened* to Mateo. And LaLa was right. Don't start talking until you have something to say. Every word means something when someone uses it, even a curse word. Filthy Jew. Dirty Mexican. White trash. Best friend. I'm sorry. Yeah, kid. Words made it okay to hate, and words made it okay to forgive. How much more power was there in the world than that?

The next time Joseph went to LaLa's house, he slipped alone into her kitchen under the pretense of getting a Coke. Stealthily, Joseph pulled out the kitchen drawer where LaLa kept a cookie tin filled with ready cash. He counted out six dollars and two cents from his wallet. He put it in the tin, covered it back, and replaced it in the drawer. He'd have paid more if he could find the Larry he hated.

42

THE HAT IN THE RING

Spring brought Passover. Brilliant-red Indian paintbrush and bluebonnets covered the sides of the roads and fields. Maman cleaned the house, fussing when she'd find bread or cookie crumbs in Joseph's bedroom. "Youssef-jun, eat in the kitchen," she pled with him. "I clean and clean, but still I find food all over the house. You and your baba . . ."

All leavened products made from flour, like bread, donuts, and cookies, had to be out of the house for the week of Passover. They'd spend the first few days at the apartment, then come home for the rest of the week. That meant Maman had two houses to clean. She tried to finish the cleaning a week ahead of time. Baba liked sweets almost as much as Joseph. Maman quit baking them in anticipation of Passover, so Baba and Joseph stashed packages of Little Debbie cakes away from Maman's sharp eyes. Joseph used to hide his sweets at LaLa's. Now that Baba was home more, it was hard to do more than pop in to change a light bulb.

The tastes, colors, and aromas of Passover lingered: crispy-crumby matzah; *halleq* made of spiced, diced apples; and nuts mixed in sweet wine and pomegranate juice. There was grassy-green parsley and scallions, sinus-blistering horseradish, and Maman's special turmeric-and-saffron matzah ball soup. Maman's Persian spices colored her meatball *gundi* burnt-orange, the color of the University of Texas. Joseph mentioned it, but she looked at him blankly. He related it to the black-and-gold colors of his football and basketball uniforms. Then she didn't understand how it related to UT's colors. By the time Joseph had explained it, the compliment was lost.

He and Shahla exchanged looks and chalked it up as a "latest." Two days after Passover, they took Shahla to the airport. It was sad to see her go before Joseph had a chance to take her riding on his dirt bike, but she couldn't afford to miss more school. Joseph promised her that he'd take her riding next time.

Baba didn't remove his kippah before they started the drive home from the Dallas airport, so Joseph wore his, too. They sang songs in Hebrew and Farsi. Maman passed around candy made from pistachios and rosewater as well as bites of almond honey cake. In true Maman fashion, she also passed around a wet washcloth to remove the stickiness from their fingers.

It was the month of Nissan, the first month of the Jewish year. It was their family name. Maybe Joseph would think less of Vonda. He could think more of the girls whose glances and smiles lingered longer now that he didn't walk Vonda to class or eat lunch with her. The trip home after Passover was a drive into a new year. It had to be better. The warm sunshine coming through the car windows made Joseph sleepy. Joseph dozed until he felt the familiar decelerations, accelerations, and turns that told him they'd reached Hazel.

Baba slowed the car a few blocks away from home. He glanced in the rearview and side mirrors. Joseph scooted up and twisted in his seat to see what Baba was watching. A car followed closely behind them. Joseph recognized Reverend Baer driving. Another car pulled in behind Reverend Baer. And then another.

Baba didn't pull in their driveway. Instead, he drove around the block. Joseph looked again. The three cars stayed close behind. His stomach pitched. Had someone seen Vonda on Joseph's dirt bike? Had she confessed that he'd kissed her? Had the reverend found their notes? How could Reverend Baer know exactly when they would return to Hazel from Dallas? A thousand unpunished sins flitted across Joseph's mind.

When Baba pulled in their driveway, he stopped short of pulling into the garage. Three cars pulled in behind them. One blocked their driveway. Two parked along the front curb. Men emerged from each car. Joseph counted nine in all. Baba got out of the car, and Maman and Joseph followed him to the front sidewalk.

"Go in the house, Miriam."

From the sound of her heels on the wooden steps and the slam of the screen door, Joseph was pretty sure she was trading her honey cake for the fireplace poker. Maman's fire exceeded her weapons.

Joseph stood with his father. He'd stand by Baba until he was ready to walk away from these overgrown thugs. It wouldn't take long.

"You, Jew-man," called Reverend Baer from the driveway. "Come here."

Baba walked forward several steps.

"I warned you about your son bothering my daughter. Now they're meeting at school, and I caught him with her in the park."

"We don't anymore, Baba. I promise," said Joseph. He took a few steps to stay close. "We don't even pass notes."

Next door, LaLa's screen door slammed. Joseph could imagine that she was standing on her porch watching. He was too fascinated and frightened to look. Abruptly, the screen door slammed again. Loudly. That could only mean one thing. She went inside to call the police. Baba had to be terrified. This was one time that Joseph wouldn't have minded LaLa wading into a fight with a yard rake and a grammatically correct lesson on the difference between good and poor manners.

"I lived in Iran until I was thirty-three years old," said Baba. "I lived there until my Muslim friend warned me the Shah's secret police want to arrest me. The government don't think a Jew able to have such a good job or make so much money. They believe that I spied for British oil company, giving away to them Iran's secrets. There was limit to how successful a Jew can be. They made up ways to take our money even if we worked hard to earn it."

Reverend Baer started to say something, but Baba cut him off. "Another Muslim friend hid me and drove my wife and me out of Tehran in middle of the night. He pass me to Christians who live in the mountains. Those Christians took us over border to other Christians in Turkey. We left everything we owned. None of those people make us pay for help."

Joseph felt pride bubbling inside him. Baba spoke with confidence, mostly correct English grammar, and hardly an accent. Joseph felt his own back straighten to match Baba's. Across the street, Mr. Ybarra emerged from under the Greers' oaks. He placed a rake in the back of his scratched pickup and picked up something else.

"Now why," asked Baba, "can Christians in Iran, who suffer the persecution like Jews, honor their Christ? And why can Muslims, who you also think infidels, have more care for human being than the man holding that baseball bat in my front yard?"

The little spring of pride became a growing stream inside Joseph, tumbling powerfully over the solid rocks of Baba's words.

Mr. Ybarra crossed the street, and he held a tire iron loosely.

Baba removed his kippah, folded it carefully, and placed it in his back pocket.

"Don't you dare preach to us, you dune goon," called out the man holding the baseball bat. Big league, not Little League. He shook the bat at Baba for emphasis.

Joseph recognized the bat man and the one who'd gotten out of the car with him. They were parents of two of the Posse who'd attacked him. He'd seen them in the school office after the fight. That was how the men knew when the Nissans would return home. The Posse boy who'd told on him to Reverend Baer was walking behind him and Alex in the hallway one day. It was the day Joseph told Alex that he'd be gone for Passover and when he'd be back. Snitch.

Baba removed his tie, rolled it, and placed it in his shirt pocket. Joseph wasn't sure why. He removed his kippah and tie, too, and stuffed them in a back pocket.

"He won't hurt you," said Reverend Baer, nodding his head toward the man with the bat. "He's just here to protect me in case you're as stubborn as your kid."

With nine grown men against one, there was no way a baseball bat was for protection.

Baba rolled up his shirtsleeves neatly. "Your friends need protecting if they step one foot in this direction," said Baba. "So do this without injure your friends also."

"Do what?" said the reverend.

"You pushed my son to the ground," said Baba. "You injure him. In Iran, a Jew endures such an insult. If I defend him, the police come. Maybe I never to be seen again. But this is America. I spoke to police about the penalty for fighting. I did arrangements to provide for my family if I go to jail. The penalty is not as bad as I feared. Maybe less for me since you come to my house with weapon. Thank you."

"You think *I'm* going to fight you?" Reverend Baer asked.

"You may refuse the fight," said Baba, "but you apologize to my son. You promise that your daughter never coming near him again."

The man with the baseball bat strode forward. Joseph held his breath, but Baba looked relaxed. Unafraid. Joseph's chest squeezed. He'd faced the Posse and a lock in a sock. A man with a bat would do way more damage. It made Joseph's head and ribs ache thinking about it. Baba had gone crazy-mad.

"Don't be afraid, Youssef," said Baba.

In his last two steps, the Posse bat man hefted the bat like a baseball player. Suddenly, Baba stepped in close. He moved gracefully, like he always did. Baba's left wrist blocked the man's left one as the bat came around. His right elbow hit the man's cheek squarely. Baba wrenched away the bat with both hands as the man fell awkwardly. Bat Man yelped in pain. Simply unbelievable.

How did Baba do that?

"Run," said Baba to the man grimacing on the ground,

holding his wrist as if it were broken. Baba pointed with the bat to the man's car. "Run now before I lose temper. I think I go to jail longer if I hurt you all. More penalty."

The man struggled up, still holding the wrist. He backed away. He seemed a little foggy about everything except the location of the baseball bat.

Mr. Ybarra walked to the man's car and opened the driver's side door helpfully. The men looked around at the noise. And the tire iron in Mr. Ybarra's hand. Mr. Ybarra pushed back his straw cowboy hat like he was about to saddle up a rambunctious young horse.

The man who'd ridden with Bat Man shook his head and guided him to the passenger side of the car. He loaded his woozy cargo into the front seat and shut the door. "It's not worth it," he said to the others. "It's just kids being kids. Maybe the raghead can afford six months in jail, but I can't." He took the driver's seat and drove off.

Mr. Ybarra tapped the calf of his leg softly with the tire iron. The reverend didn't seem like the type to pick on someone his own size. That left six against two. Counting Joseph, it was six against three. Based on what Joseph had just seen, Baba could take on two or three of them and come out okay. Mr. Ybarra was tough from long hours of hard work. Maman might pop out the front door with a fireplace poker at any time. LaLa's yard rake wouldn't be far behind. It looked pretty even. Way better than it looked in the eighth-grade hallway with the Posse Comitatus.

"I'm not apologizing to anyone," said Reverend Baer. "But I have warned Vonda to stay away from your filthy son."

In the distance, a siren wailed. Baba flinched, but he stood his ground. It was Reverend Baer who looked uncomfortable.

Maybe it wasn't a good thing for preachers to go around threatening people. Joseph had met LaLa's preacher several times. He would never do something like that.

"My son will be the mayor of this town someday," said Mr. Ybarra softly, interrupting the high-voltage silence. "He respects everyone in this community. In twenty years, we will be old men, but our children will be young. Reverend, our grandchildren will learn about people like you in books, not on sidewalks and in public streets. They will be ashamed of men like you. But of men like Mr. Nissan, they will be proud. And of my sons and Joseph, they will be proud. I am proud of them already." The police car sounded as if it was only a block away. Mr. Ybarra faded back to his pickup, got in, and drove away.

A patrol car pulled up to the curb. Its siren faded to a long moan and went silent. A policeman stepped out. He was dressed in a neatly ironed navy-blue uniform, patent-leather shoes and duty belt, and a heavy revolver hung on his hip. He took a long look around before he asked, "What's the problem here, gentlemen?"

LaLa's screen door slammed again. A witness. Maybe Baba wouldn't have to go to jail.

"We were just leaving, Officer Oliver," said Reverend Baer.

"I should hope so," said the officer. "Any report I write on this will start with seven churchgoing men all blown up like fightin' roosters in a Jewish man's yard while he stands there with his little boy. Coincidentally, he's the only Jewish man in the county. Will I be writing a report today?"

"I want no trouble," said Baba.

"What happened, son?" the policeman asked Joseph.

"These men are mad at me because I was friends with the

reverend's daughter," said Joseph. "I'm Jewish." He didn't know what else to add. That pretty much summed it up.

"Say, aren't you Joseph? Don't you play football with my son, Jimmy Oliver?" asked the officer. He didn't mention that he already knew Joseph from the Edmondson investigation.

"Yes, sir," said Joseph. "We both play defense."

Officer Oliver said, "I'm chairman of the high school football booster club. We're real excited about your playing on the high school team next year. The coaches can't stop talking about you and Garza. I'm hoping to drop in on spring training next week to see how you're coming along."

Without being told, Reverend Baer and the others got back in their cars, started them, and drove away. You had to love the power of football in Texas.

"If you think there will be more trouble, you can come down and sign your complaint," Officer Oliver said to Baba. "I still have it in my desk. We can update it."

Joseph couldn't believe his ears. *Baba* went to the *police*?

"I have no complaining," said Baba. He handed the officer the bat. "One of them dropped this."

"Dropped it?"

"It looked like he stumbled," said Baba with a perfectly straight face.

Officer Oliver studied the bat. "Is he okay?"

"I believe his wrist broke. And perhaps his face hit my elbow when I tried to help him not to fall. I picked up the bat so he won't hit himself in the head with it."

Joseph had to turn away to control his expression. Who was this man?

The officer didn't bother stifling his grin. LaLa beckoned

from her front porch. In her other hand was the infallible yard rake. "Excuse me," said Officer Oliver. He walked to Miss Eleanor's and spent several minutes talking to her.

Baba and Joseph climbed their front porch steps and sat on the porch swing. Baba replaced his kippah and tie before he unrolled his sleeves and buttoned them. "How did you learn how to do that, Baba?" Joseph asked.

Baba patted Joseph on the knee. "I said that in Iran, Jews were not permitted to learn self-defense. I never said I didn't learn anyway. Your uncles were good teachers."

When Miss Eleanor's screen door banged again, Joseph looked over. Officer Oliver walked back to the patrol car. He put the baseball bat in the back seat. With a wave, he started the car and pulled away.

43

NEWSBOY CAP

Joseph sleepily removed his prayer tefillin and put them in their velvet bag. Baba was home this week, so they'd prayed together. Afterward, Joseph went to get his book bag for school. When Joseph sat down to breakfast, a folded *Hazel Herald* newspaper lay beside his plate. The paper was folded so an article was faceup.

Two local brothers, Terry and Vernon Edmondson, pled guilty yesterday on several criminal counts following a plea deal in circuit court. The brothers were part of a drug ring transporting marijuana and cocaine from Texas border towns to Dallas. From there, the drugs were distributed to surrounding states. Firearms were moved to Mexico along the same distribution route.

In exchange for reduced sentences, the Edmondsons pled guilty to charges of: conspiracy to possess marijuana with intent to distribute, conspiracy to import

marijuana, unlawful distribution of controlled sub-
stances, conspiracy to possess cocaine with intent to
distribute, conspiracy to import cocaine, conspiracy to
possess firearms in furtherance of drug trafficking, and
possession of a firearm by a convicted felon.

Charges of common nuisance, possession of drug
paraphernalia, and contributing to the delinquency
of a minor were dropped. Both defendants were in
violation of parole on previous convictions. Charges
are pending in federal district court on charges of
transporting a controlled substance with intent to
distribute across state lines and transporting stolen
firearms across state lines. Sentencing in the case is
set for late May.

"Contributing to the delinquency of a minor." Was Brian's
dad making him sell the drugs? But Larry was a year older. He
was fifteen. Why not him?

It dawned on Joseph. Grimy Boy. Dirty Bird. That's how
he thought of Larry. Brian wasn't a shining example of personal
hygiene, but Larry's grimy fingernails, hat, and sneakers . . . the
mounds of fresh earth . . . Could Larry have been forced to help
dig the hidden drug room? He was much stronger than Brian.
Larry was always clean in school, so he wasn't just a dirty kid.
And he'd disappeared. Maybe he was afraid of going to juvy.

Joseph could see Baba's relief. There was almost a smile when
he sipped his tea. By pleading guilty, the Edmondsons made it
unnecessary for Joseph and Roberto to testify in court. The less
contact with police, the better for Baba. He'd faced his worst

fear, but Baba would probably never want to go to the court-
house again for anything except to renew his driver's license.

There was more to the Iranian escape story than Baba and
Maman were telling. Why not just ask Baba outright? He was
certainly in a good mood.

"Baba?"

"What is it, *Aziz-am?*"

"Why are you so afraid of the police? What really happened
in Iran?"

Maman turned sharply from the kitchen sink. She stared at
them both in some sort of fiery horror. He'd seen her fire, yes,
willing to fight the night boo on their porch with a poker. This
was different. It was a helpless fury, like a red needle spinning
around a thermometer.

A cold, dark seriousness settled upon Baba.

"*Nah*, Kamran," Maman pled softly. Her whole body was
taut. Rage. Control. Baba glanced at her, but Joseph knew
Baba would do whatever he wanted no matter how many times
she said no. Baba turned his head and looked out the kitchen
window for a long time. "*Nah*, Kamran," Maman begged again.

"He should know," replied Baba.

Maman abruptly threw a saucepan into the sink. Suds flew
up. The bubbles stuck to the cabinets and landed on the countertop. "Miriam . . ." said Baba. She ignored him and flung the
wet dishrag across the room at him. When she yanked open the
back door and went outside, she slammed it so hard the windows
rattled. Maybe Baba was right about the temper coming from
her side of the family. The Piggly Wiggly cashier better watch
her apples.

A silent minute passed. Through the window, Joseph saw

Maman back the car out of the driveway. She did it much faster than she normally did. When she drove off, it was with purpose.

"Youssef," Baba said, "you must never repeat this to anyone. Do you promise?"

"*Baleh*, Baba," said Joseph.

"I killed two police officers in Tehran."

Joseph's heart skipped a beat.

"If anyone comes for me, you must hide Maman. Take her to her relatives in Israel, not Los Angeles. If they find me here, they'd find her in LA. Israel is dangerous, but it will be safer for you both in her family's neighborhood. Take her to one of those airport cities I showed you. She can withdraw our money to live on. Do you promise me?"

Joseph had to swallow several times to make his throat work right. Finally, he managed, "*Baleh*, Baba."

"Thank you, *Aziz-am*. It was self-defense. I'd have never done it otherwise, but they wanted to kill me and imprison Maman. Maybe they'd kill her, too, but only after they violated and tortured her for information about her brother. No one would be able to help her. I know you think I'm a coward, but I hate killing. I hate even striking someone. Spanking you was the hardest thing I've ever done. I knew it would hurt you so deeply that you'd always think twice about fighting."

"But, Baba, it looked so easy when you knocked down that man in our front yard . . ."

"Yes, Youssef, but none of those men wanted to face me alone. They brought nine men," said Baba.

"It's because you're so big."

"That's only part of the reason. So many came because no matter how much I despise hurting someone, I will do it if it's the last option. I spanked you, Youssef, because you thought fighting was a first option. When you are willing to harm someone, they sense it. You fought two boys at the store, not one. Many boys attacked you at school, not one. You understand?" asked Baba.

"Not exactly," said Joseph.

"I took you to boxing class so that you had the training to be willing. So people would hesitate to harm you. When you are *willing*, it makes people less eager to test whether you *will*. But you must control your temper. You are *too* willing."

Joseph understood. Kind of.

Baba continued, "Maybe the Shah's government people who wanted to take revenge on us are out of power. Maybe they are running for their own lives now. We might fade from their memories."

"I don't think you're a coward, Baba. I understand now."

Baba gave him a glance. It was sad, disbelieving. It must have been a heavy burden to bear.

44

HANG UP YOUR HAT

Joseph stared at Maman's copy of Persian poetry that lay open before him. He and Baba had argued that morning. Bad. The chair rental company dropped off the chairs for Miss Eleanor's piano recital late. They stacked them at the bottom of her porch and drove off. Joseph walked over to move them inside her parlor, but Baba called him back. It was Shabbat. Joseph had no business carrying chairs on Shabbat. The students could set them up. She could call the rental place to come finish the job.

No, Joseph had argued. Miss Eleanor would never allow a recital to start without every chair, program, cookie tray, and lemonade pitcher in place. It was beneath her dignity to ask the students and parents to set up folding chairs. It was too hard on her knees to go up and down the porch steps that many times. Instead of giving up, Joseph had said things. Baba had said things. Maman looked as if she were watching a fatal car wreck. Joseph went to his room and slammed the door. Maman's side of the family.

Joseph flipped through the book, looking bitterly at the lines he'd translated and copied for Vonda.

Your love should never be offered to the mouth of a
  stranger,
Only to someone who has the courage and bravery
To cut pieces of his soul off with a knife
Then weave them into a blanket to protect you.

Vonda had shrugged off the blanket of his soul and left it in a tree house. She hadn't looked back when she walked away in the park. Sure, she'd said she was sorry. That's what you say when you want to get rid of someone kindly.

Joseph read another line of the poet Hafiz:

People say that when the soul heard the song of
  creation, it entered the body,
but actually, the soul itself was the song.

Hafiz's nickname was the Tongue of the Invisible. That summed up Joseph's time with Vonda. Invisible. Joseph would never know what she really thought of him. Was he a curiosity, a real Jew just like she read about in Sunday school? Was it his nice clothes? Whatever it was, she'd never intended to disappoint her father with a brown Jewish boy. She was happiest with Joseph when they were pen pals.

The image of Fereshteh came to him, the beautiful girl who sat with Shahla. Copper eyes smiled at him. Then the image of the sad Fereshteh replaced it, the one he pushed away and humiliated. He hadn't gotten rid of her kindly. She'd be stuck in his soul forever. A mistake he'd never be able to correct. Would she always share the humiliation of that moment with him, like the faded chalk of Yom Kippur, or would it completely erase? Sometimes in a nightmare, Joseph did something horrible, and it was a relief to wake up and know he didn't really do it, that he wouldn't go to jail. The nightmare soon faded unless he dreamed it again. What he said to Fereshteh was real, though. It just wouldn't fade.

If there were songs in Joseph's soul, he'd never play them on LaLa's piano. No matter what he'd said to Baba, in the end, he was a Jew and a Persian. The distance between Iran and Texas proved you never really fit in either place. Each side thought you were theirs. Farsi and English never quite translated except in road signs that didn't need translating. Joseph would always be in the middle. Today, though, his soul would sing one last song. To Texas ladies, one soft kiss, and foolish, hopeful notes. To accepting things stuck in a bottle. To suffering and silence.

Baba looked up from his recliner when Joseph walked through the living room. Joseph dropped his tie over his upturned collar. "Where are you going, Youssef?" Baba asked, his words aflame. Baba was still angry. Joseph knew more about Baba than ever before, but they were farther apart.

"Miss Eleanor's."

"Youssef-jun, do not defy your father," pled Maman. "Miss Eleanor understands you can't come over to play piano."

"I'll be back in thirty minutes," said Joseph.

"Youssef, go to your room," Baba said, rising from the recliner.

"*Nah*, Baba."

Baba's face turned red. Joseph turned down his collar over

the tie and gave it a final tug. "I'm going to Miss Eleanor's to play in the recital."

"No, you're not," said Baba, moving to block the front door. "You've never played on a Shabbat, and you won't start now."

"You can't stop me," said Joseph.

Joseph tried to shoulder past Baba, but his father grabbed his right arm. Maman desperately grabbed his left hand. With a quick, violent twist, Joseph broke free and backed toward the door. "You can't stop me," he repeated. "So let me go."

Baba advanced, but Joseph flashed him a look. Baba hesitated. Maman's side of the family.

"Thirty minutes," Joseph repeated. He plucked a yellow rose from the vase of Shabbat flowers, went out the front door, and down the front walk.

A Schumann piece drifted from Miss Eleanor's open parlor window. Joseph knew Miss Eleanor was sitting in the front row of rented folding chairs, and he knew what she was thinking. He'd heard her say different versions of it over the past eight years: "Dear, this is a piano, not a typewriter. A pianist is a translator for a composer, giving meaning to what the composer intended. Music doesn't require a secretary to type its obituary; it begs a pianist to give it articulation, dynamics, *rubato, tempi!*"

Joseph grasped the cut Shabbat rose in his hand so hard that the thorns pricked his fingers. He used the kitchen entrance and waited until the ripple of polite applause excused the last terrified student from the piano bench.

Joseph adjusted his kippah, flexed his fingers, and strode into the parlor. His dress shoes struck the wooden floor boldly. "Miss Eleanor," he said, and bowed slightly, offering the rose.

She took it, and he walked to the bench. Joseph leveled a long, fearless look at Reverend Baer. Vonda squirmed in her seat.

Joseph wasn't on the program, but Miss Eleanor hid her surprise. Always a Texas lady. "Joseph Nissan," she said, "will be playing . . ."

"Brahms's Intermezzo in A major," Joseph inserted.

". . . to finish our recital today." Miss Eleanor's uplifted eyebrow betrayed her. It was a most difficult piece, rarely selected, but her favorite. It moved the strings of her soul.

It was Joseph's first and last recital. Through the open window, Joseph could see Maman and Baba standing on their front porch looking toward Miss Eleanor's house. He pulled out the bench, sat, and played. He played like he'd never played before. He imitated no one. Joseph translated the Brahms chromatic harmony into his own apology, gratefulness, sorrow, love, and kind farewell. The keys yielded to his brown fingers like the soft flesh of Vonda's white hands once had.

The slow, defiant notes filled the parlor, spilled out the window, rolled over the hydrangeas, and marched up the steps to his own front porch. Tiny crimson smudges from the thorns pressed onto the ivory keys. Joseph glanced through the window again. Baba and Maman sat together on the porch swing.

When the last note echoed through the acoustic wooden wonder of the old house, Joseph ran a finger noiselessly one last time across the keys, wiping away a few smudges of blood. Tiny drops of a soul. He looked up at the old fiddle on the wall, tears streaming down his cheeks. "I'll miss you," he whispered. He looked over at Miss Eleanor. No one clapped, coughed, or moved. Softly, she rapped one time on the chair beside her.

Joseph pressed his hand over his heart: "A beautiful song for a beautiful lady, Miss Eleanor."

Youssef Nissan stood and slid the bench under the piano. He bent to kiss Miss Eleanor's wrinkled, wet cheeks twice, Persian style. It was a short walk home. No need to check. His kippah was clipped on straight.

45
RECAP

Joseph hummed the notes to the Torah page open before him Friday afternoon. School was out. They were staying at the Dallas apartment overnight for Shabbat. Sunday morning, Joseph, Shahla, and Maman would fly to Israel to visit relatives. Thankfully, Baba dropped the threat of sending Joseph to attend a religious school in Israel. Joseph no longer worried about it being a one-way ticket. Shahla and Maman had finished preparing the evening meal and showered, and now they took turns braiding one another's hair. Their little world free of his and Baba's intrusion.

Pulling open his gym bag, Joseph pulled a slip of paper from the inside pocket. Roberto had found the paper in his riding jacket in early spring. He gave it to Joseph without comment. Joseph put the paper beside the open Torah.

"Canon in Me"

Youssef
I play the piano

The piano plays me
I play the daughter
The daughter plays me.
I play life
Life plays me
And I play dead
Joseph

You couldn't hum it to the tune of "Yellow Rose of Texas." Like Vonda, the words were a mystery. Was it her apology? Despair? Words written thousands of years ago were easier to understand.

The Hebrew words on the page were ancient. Joseph resented the rabbi's latest comment about Baba's pronunciation of the text. Baba's way was truer to ancient Hebrew. Baba would do it his way, and the rabbi would deal with it. That's just the way it was. The poem and a crumpled receipt for six dollars and two cents went back into the gym bag. Maybe someday Joseph would understand them. A kid couldn't be expected to translate everything in life.

Like Miss Eleanor said about Baba, Vonda and Larry had hard burdens. Everyone has a cat in the hat. A bicycle, peach ice cream, and a kippah tossed Joseph's life into the air, and he'd landed in a new place. People change. Some for better, some for worse. When people change, things change. That's the shining sun and the star-blue sky. That's the danger and the night boos. And that's the burden.

Joseph reached again into his gym bag. He removed an Out of Order sign and two packages of stink bait. There were advantages to living in a rural Texas town. Bait-and-tackle shops were one of them. Joseph slid the sign and packages into a plastic bag and sealed it. It fit nicely into his tallit bag for the walk to the synagogue for evening prayers.

Rabbi Rothstein wouldn't be enjoying his private restroom on Shabbat. His latest snide comment to Baba was one comment too many. By the time the rabbi figured out nothing was wrong with the toilet, the stink bait would do its work in the tiny space. Joseph would be on a plane somewhere over the Atlantic Ocean. Even if the rabbi figured out who did it, Joseph didn't think Baba would mind.

Fly high. Family stick together.

ACKNOWLEDGMENTS

Thanks to my agent Steven, who found the best place to hang *The Hat* for readers of all ages. Thanks to his diligence, the world can hear about more than just the recipes of the Mizrachi Jews, who remain second-class citizens in communities where one should least expect it. Although it's been nearly a lifetime since we parted, thanks also to my LaLa, may her memory be for blessing, who welcomed a dark-skinned Persian girl into the community. I still have that photo of you holding me, standing next to my birthday cake. To my cousin, thank you for being a big brother and protector when we were young outsiders. I only ever remember being the recipient of your kindness.